WILDFIRE

Track Record

Race through all the Wildfire
original novels

Show-off
Track Record

Coming soon: *Riding Lessons*

WILDFIRE

Track Record

An original novel by Catherine Hapka

Based on the series created by Michael Piller & Christopher Teague

DISNEP PRESS

New York

Copyright © 2006 Lions Gate Television Inc.

First Published by Disney Press in 2007
Printed in the United States of America

First Edition
1 3 5 7 9 10 8 6 4 2

Library of Congress Catalog Card Number: 2005938558
ISBN 1-4231-0189-8

Cover design by Alfred Giuliani
Interior design by Arlene Schleifer Goldberg

Visit www.abcfamily.com/wildfire

WILDFIRE

Track Record

Chapter One

It doesn't get better than this, Kris Furillo thought, her eyes glued to the sight unfolding in front of her. A magnificent bay Thoroughbred swept around an almost-empty track, his ears back and his neck stretched forward. Kris felt her smile grow bigger as she watched Wildfire's legs pump faster and faster, until they were little more than a blur in the hazy early morning light. Crouched over the horse's saddle, the exercise rider's hands were buried in the flying black mane, letting Wildfire do exactly what centuries of breeding had prepared him to do: run.

For a moment, Kris felt as if she were living some fantastic dream. Could this really be *her* life? Taking her eyes off Wildfire for just a moment, she shot a quick glance at the five people standing around her at the rail, and then at the colorful expanse of the racetrack surrounding them.

There is no arguing, she thought gleefully. My life is definitely a dream come true. And I know I mostly have Pablo Betart to thank for that—and Wildfire, of course.

Kris had met both of them soon after arriving at Camp LaGrange, the prison camp where she'd been sent after getting mixed up in a car theft in her hometown of Oakland, California. Before LaGrange, Kris had barely even seen a horse up close, let alone ridden one. But the camp offered a work program at the local police-horse training facility that gave her the chance to get out of the drab confines of the prison camp once in a while. She had jumped at the chance and figured the needed horse sense would come with time.

And boy, had it been a good decision. After all, she had met Wildfire. The horse had captured her attention from the first moment she'd seen him. Younger and more reactive than the majority of the police-horse trainees, who were mostly staid, bombproof quarter horse and draft cross geldings, Wildfire was a handful. He was also a lot like Kris: confused by how he'd ended up where he was and with no idea of how to make things better for himself. The two had instantly bonded and, despite her lack of experience, Kris was soon riding him around the training facility's ring as if she'd been in the saddle all her life.

Pablo hadn't made the same kind of dramatic impression on Kris at the beginning, though his effect on her life had been equally great in the end. He helped the officers train the horses, and his keen horseman's eye had spotted Kris's potential right away. Carefully and patiently he had helped her shape her skills whenever they worked together. And when the time came for Kris to leave Camp LaGrange, Pablo had ensured that she would have somewhere to go other than back to her rough, dead-end old neighborhood in Oakland. He had offered her a place at Raintree Horse Farm.

When he wasn't volunteering at the police

training center, Pablo was the manager and head trainer at Raintree. The Thoroughbred breeding and racing facility was owned by Jean Ritter, an energetic woman with an intense love of horses running through her veins. Pablo had convinced Jean to give Kris a chance, and before long Kris—and Wildfire—were settling into their new home on the sprawling ranch.

The transition hadn't been easy for either of them. But slowly, Kris had grown more comfortable in her new life, and with the other people on the ranch. Jean's father, Henry Ritter, was always doling out good advice and telling Kris stories of the farm's glory days. And Todd, Jean's youngest son, had been her number one supporter from the beginning. In fact, every member of the Ritter family made her feel comfortable. Well, *almost* everyone. The oldest son, Matt, was around Kris's age, and from the start, an intense attraction had flared between them.

At first, Kris had been inclined to follow her feelings and see where things went with Matt. But she'd quickly realized it was not going to be that easy. After all, Matt was the son of her employer, and it hadn't been hard to see that Jean disapproved of the two of them becoming anything more than friends. Besides that, Matt wasn't like other guys Kris had known, and she had no clue how to handle him. He wasn't a petty criminal or a chauvinistic pig. He was sweet and kind and utterly charming. Because of all that, Kris had decided it was better to keep things platonic. But, she had to admit, that was often easier said than done.

Despite that tension, after several months on the ranch Kris was happier there than anywhere she'd ever been. And while a lot had to do with the Ritters, it was mostly because of Wildfire. . . .

Turning away from the grandstand, Kris brought her full attention back to the horse on the track just in time to see him pass one of the brightly striped poles that marked out distances on the track. Beside her, she heard a soft click even above the clapping and talking of the people. Glancing over, she saw Pablo staring down at his stopwatch.

"How'd he do?" Henry asked from his spot on the rail.

"One-oh-nine and change," Pablo replied.

Matt, who was also standing near the rail, let out a low whistle. "Nice," he said. "A time like that could win half the races on the card at six furlongs."

Kris felt her heart swell with pride. Just about the only thing that would have made this moment better was if *she* were the one riding Wildfire out there, as she normally did when he trained back home at the ranch. But that was not going to happen . . . yet. Pablo wanted the jockey who would ride Wildfire when, and if, he raced to get to know him. So, Kris had reluctantly given up the training ride for a little while. Secretly, she dreamed of becoming a licensed jockey herself, maybe even riding Wildfire to victory one day in big races like the Santa Anita Derby or the Sandpiper Classic. But, for now, it was enough just to watch him and know that she'd played a role in bringing him to this moment.

Even though he was naturally talented and loved to run, Wildfire had struggled with some aspects of his race training, including breaking from the starting gate. But he seemed to be over most of that now, which was why Pablo had made the decision to move him to the track and train him there for a while.

"Do you think he'll be ready to race soon?" Kris asked Pablo with some trepidation.

The trainer shrugged, his eyes never leaving Wildfire as he continued to gallop around the far turn. "We'll see," he said. "It may be time to start thinking about it."

Coming from Pablo, who could be as conservative and tight-lipped as anyone Kris had ever known, that was a bold statement. Kris felt like whooping with joy, but instead she settled for trading a smile and a wink with Matt.

Out on the track, the jockey brought Wildfire down to a canter, then a trot. As they turned and jogged back toward the gap leading to the stable area, the handsome bay colt held his head high, blowing a bit but still prancing energetically even after the brisk workout.

"Looks like he's feeling good. I'd better go help untack him for the hot-walker," Pablo said, already taking a few steps toward the gap.

"Need a hand?" Kris asked, hurrying after him.

Pablo shook his head. "I've got it covered," he said with a smile. "You stay here and have fun."

As Pablo disappeared into the crowd, Kris wandered back to the others, hoping to talk about Wildfire's prospects now that his training was coming along so well. But she found that they'd already changed the subject.

". . . and then there was that gray pony, the one Mom tried to turn into a trick horse for the movies," Matt was saying. "Todd, do you remember? You were pretty young then."

"I remember!" Todd laughed. "His name was Stevie, right?"

"Right!" Henry slapped his knee and chortled, his eyes sparkling. "We named him after your cousin Steve from Arizona, since he was always tripping over his own feet, too. Remember the scene he made at Charlotte's wedding?"

"You mean cousin Steve, not that pony, right?" Matt quipped.

Jean chuckled. Then, suddenly noticing Kris standing there, she reached out and patted her on the arm. "Oh, Kris," she said.

"Sorry. You must be wondering what we're talking about—see, there was this nutty pony my ex-husband picked up at auction. . . ."

Kris smiled politely through Jean's explanation, which sent Matt, Todd, and Henry into renewed peals of laughter and chatter about other eccentric horses and family members. But inside, she was cringing. She didn't have funny family stories or warm memories of old ponies. Instead, she just had memories of a mother who couldn't take care of herself, let alone her daughter, and nights on the street.

How would I even know if these people are starting to feel like family? she wondered with a sudden pang of self-pity. I mean, I like them, and I'm pretty sure they like me. But family? It's not like I've ever really had experience with that sort of thing. . . .

Clearing her throat, she suddenly felt the need to be by herself for a little while. "I'll be back in a bit," she said, trying to sound normal. "I—I want to go grab a cup of coffee." Shooting them a fake yawn, she turned and hurried off as the others continued their conversation, unaware of her angst.

Once she was away from the Ritters, Kris relaxed. Even though the rest of the world was still sleeping, the day was already well under way at the racetrack. Kris loved the excitement of post time later in the day, when the public poured into the grandstand to cheer on the glossy, muscled horses and the jockeys in their colorful silks. But she was starting to like early mornings at the track even more. Smiling, she wandered farther into the backside area, where the horses stabled at the track lived.

Backside, there was a different kind of excitement in the air, an energy that went with the hard work of preparing horses to race. Kris ducked to the side of the path as a lanky gray colt pranced past at the end of his lead rope, his feet flying and nostrils flaring. Nearby, a dark bay mare stood quietly as a groom hosed her off after a workout. Other workers hurried past, lugging tack or bales of hay, while several trainers wandered around, talking on cell phones or consulting training charts.

For a moment Kris thought about heading to the shedrow where Wildfire was stabled, but she quickly decided against it. Pablo would only wonder why she hadn't stayed with the Ritters as he'd ordered—and Pablo was a lot harder to fool than the others. She just didn't feel like getting involved in a conversation about how she was or wasn't fitting in.

Instead, she wandered down the nearest shedrow, admiring the horses behind the Dutch doors or the webbed stall guards. Some were dozing, others were picking at hay that hung in nets outside their doors, and the rest were pacing in their stalls or standing and watching what was going on outside.

Near the end of the aisle, one horse in particular caught her eye. He was a big chestnut colt with a broad, white blaze and kind eyes. His head was massive yet somehow still elegant, and well-defined muscles rippled in the neck and shoulders beneath his sleek coat. The stall door was open, and the colt was standing calmly behind a single chain stall guard, enjoying the breeze from the small electric fan clipped to the door frame.

"Wow," Kris breathed, stepping toward the horse. While she usually only had eyes for Wildfire, this horse was unbelievable. He was the definition of pure Thoroughbred. As she moved within range of the fan, the few strands of her long, dark hair that had escaped from her ponytail blew into her face. Reaching up, she pushed them back without taking her eyes off the chestnut colt. "Did anybody ever tell you you're gorgeous?"

Even though she knew better—after all, she didn't know this horse or its owners—she couldn't resist taking another step forward and touching the wide blaze on the chestnut's nose. He snuffled at her hand eagerly. Laughing, she patted him on his glossy neck.

"Isn't he a sweetie?" a voice said from behind her. "You'd never know from looking at him now that he set the track record at seven furlongs just last month."

Kris jumped. She had been caught! Spinning around, she faced the speaker, a petite woman in her early twenties with a round, friendly face sprinkled with reddish brown freckles that matched her short, wavy hair.

"Sorry," Kris blurted out. "I—I know I shouldn't go around petting random racehorses. I mean, I'm not a total idiot."

The young woman laughed. "Don't sweat it," she said. "Nobody can resist stopping to pat Beau. It's like he sends out these beams of friendliness that no one can resist."

Kris smiled, relieved. "Cool," she said. "So, is he yours? I mean, are you Beau's trainer, or his jockey, or . . ."

"Groom. Well, not *his* groom, but *a* groom. I'm Melina. I work for Trenton Stables. Jeff Trenton is Beau's trainer."

Kris nodded, impressed. She'd heard of Trenton—he was one of the most successful trainers in the region. His business was busy enough that he had several assistant trainers working for him at different area tracks.

"Working for Jeff Trenton," Kris mused. "Wow, that must be a great job."

Melina shrugged. "Pays the bills," she said lightly. "How about you? I don't remember seeing you around. You work on the backside, or just visiting?"

"Oh!" Blushing, Kris realized she hadn't even introduced herself. "Some of each, actually. I work for Raintree Horse Farm—we run here pretty often. My name's Kris Furillo."

Melina's hazel eyes immediately lit up with recognition. "Get out!" she cried. "*The* Kris Furillo? Like, the runaway, life-risking, horse-saving Kris Furillo?"

Kris wasn't sure whether to feel embarrassed or flattered by Melina's obvious delight. It was easy to forget that almost everyone west of the Rockies had watched on live TV as she'd galloped Wildfire across the desert, away from the low-end auction where he'd ended up after flunking out of his police-horse training, chased by police cars and helicopters. "That's me," she said. "But I don't go around doing crazy stuff like that all the time or anything."

"You don't have to explain it to me." Melina smiled and gave Beau a scratch on the withers. "Trust me, if someone tried to send Beau or any of my guys to auction, I'd be saddling up and riding off into the desert, too."

"Yeah," Kris agreed. "Wildfire was worth it. He's pretty special."

"That's what I've heard." Melina said, shooting her an admiring glance. "I also heard you've been helping train him."

"Sort of." Kris shrugged her shoulders

and tried to downplay it. "I mean, Pablo . . ."

"Pablo Betart, right? Isn't he the head dude at Raintree?" Melina interrupted. "Jackson—that's our head groom—he says Pablo's one of the best." She shrugged. "I guess they've known each other a long time."

It was a hard fact to miss—Pablo seemed to know *everybody* in the racing business. "He's taught me everything I know," she admitted. "Well, him and Wildfire, that is."

"I hear you," Melina said with a laugh. "My best teacher ever was this ornery old track pony named Justice. . . ."

The two of them chatted for a few more minutes and Kris felt herself relaxing in a way she hadn't in years. After keeping everyone at a distance, she couldn't help liking Melina right away. It was nice to talk to someone close to her own age who clearly felt just as strongly about horses as she did.

In the middle of describing the funny habits of one of her charges, Melina suddenly cut herself off by glancing at her watch. "Oh, kick me in the head!" she exclaimed. "I was supposed to start tacking up Khan ten minutes ago."

"Oh." Kris couldn't help suddenly feeling disappointed. Was Melina blowing her off? "Sorry to hold you up."

Melina turned and hurried a few steps off down the shedrow. Then, pausing, she glanced back over her shoulder. "Hey, if you're not doing anything right now, want to help me out?" she asked. "The K-man can be a handful; I could totally use the help if you don't mind."

Smiling, Kris nodded. "Right behind you."

Chapter Two

"Yo, big Mac!" Melina called out as they passed a short, slender young man. "That black colt dump you again? When are you gonna learn to ride?"

Kris noticed that the young man had dirt on his pants and sleeves and was walking a bit gingerly. But at Melina's words, he grinned and flashed her a wave. "I'll learn to ride the same time you learn to paint a hoof without painting half the barn at the same time, Mel," he called back.

"Sounds like a plan," Melina replied easily. She glanced at Kris. "Kris, this obnoxious dude here is Mac Mackenzie. He rides for us. Tries to, at least. Mac, this is Kris. She's the girl who's training that Wildfire colt for the Ritters over at Raintree."

"I'm not really *training* him," Kris protested as the exercise rider looked at her with interest.

"Who's not training whom?" a new voice broke in from behind Kris and Melina.

Turning, Kris saw a well-dressed man in his late twenties standing with one hand on his hip. Slightly built and a little shorter than Kris, he was handsome in a sharp-featured sort of way. His spotless khakis, polo shirt, and leather loafers stood out beside the messier, more casual clothes the others were wearing, and his blond hair was gelled into a stylish do.

"Oh, hi, Parker," Melina said.

Kris glanced curiously over at her new friend. Her attitude had done a complete one-eighty. Melina's voice had lost its playful, sarcastic edge and gone sort of soft and gooey around the edges.

Parker smiled briefly at her, then turned his attention to Mac. "You finished with the black colt?" he barked. "I just sent Joey to the track looking for you. I'll be there in a minute to watch you ride that new filly from the East Coast."

Mac nodded, then hurried off in the direction he'd come. Melina was still gazing at Parker.

"Hey, Parker, this is Kris Furillo from Raintree," she said, gesturing vaguely in Kris's direction. "Kris, this is Parker Williams. He's the assistant trainer in charge of the Trenton horses at this track."

Kris nodded politely, doing her best to hide her amused smile. It was pretty obvious that Melina was nursing a big-time crush on her boss. "Hi," she said. "Nice to meet you."

"Likewise," Parker said, though he barely spared Kris a quick smile before consulting his watch. "Melina, José just brought back that pair of babies who got here yesterday. Get over there and help him untack, okay?"

"Sure thing," Melina said as eagerly as if he'd just ordered her to take the rest of the day off.

Following Melina down the shedrow, they found a heavyset, harassed-looking older groom wrestling with a pair of sweaty, unruly two-year-old colts. Kris quickly grabbed one of the horses and walked him off a little ways, doing her best to settle him, while Melina helped pull the saddle off the second.

"Ready for this guy yet?" Kris called, turning her charge in a circle and doing her best to avoid his teeth as he tried to nip at her hand, the lead rope, and anything else that happened to pass in front of his muzzle.

"Bring him over," Melina shouted.

"I got him," the groom, José, said gruffly in a thick Spanish accent. "Don't let him bite you. He's a mouthy one."

As he pulled the tack off Kris's colt, a very tall, very skinny young man with a prominent Adam's apple appeared around the corner of the shedrow. "Oh, there y'all are," he said in a low voice tinged with a warm, Southern accent. "I was lookin' for you."

"Shorty! Where have you been?" José exclaimed, before launching into a torrent of Spanish.

"Easy, José," Melina broke in. "Shorty's here now, and that's what matters." Tossing the lead shank of the horse she was holding to the tall newcomer, she added, "Here you go. Be careful with this one—he's definitely feeling his oats!"

"Okay, Melina." Shorty tugged gently on the lead and gave the colt a pat. "I'm sure we'll git along just fine."

As he wandered off with the colt in tow, Melina stepped over to help Kris, who was still playing keep-away with her hands and the second colt's teeth. "That was Shorty," Melina explained. "He hot-walks for us. Drives us crazy 'cause he's always late or lost in space. But the horses love him. Apparently, they find him very soothing."

As José went to put away the tack, Melina and Kris tracked down another hot-walker to take the remaining colt off their hands. Just as the horse danced off and disappeared around the end of the shedrow, another groom appeared with a list of chores for Melina from Parker.

"The excitement never stops around here," Melina said, glancing at Kris. "By the way, you really don't have to stick around and help me if you're bored or whatever."

Kris shrugged. "If there's one word I'd never use to describe this place, it's boring," she said. "I totally don't mind helping. So, what are we doing next?"

Even though a lot of the chores were the same ones she had to do daily back at Raintree, helping Melina with her job felt different . . . more useful somehow. It's like I belong, Kris thought as she followed Melina around. No one sees me as an ex-con or charity case. They see me as a horse person. A *good* horse person. Smiling, she picked up her pace to keep up with Melina. It was turning into a great day.

A few minutes later, Kris was standing in the aisle holding a young filly's lead shank and scratching her on the jaw while Melina wrapped her legs. Suddenly, she heard someone calling her name. Looking up, she saw Matt hurrying toward them.

"There you are," Matt said when he reached her. "I've been looking everywhere for you."

"Sorry." Kris smiled at him sheepishly. "Guess I kind of lost track of time."

Straightening up, Melina wiped her hands on her jeans and took a long look at Matt.

"Hey, Kris," she said playfully. "Who's your cute friend?"

"This is Matt," Kris replied, trying not to blush. She knew Matt was cute, but hated to be reminded considering how *bad* an idea it was to think so. "Matt Ritter. Matt, this is Melina. She works for Trenton Stables."

"Trenton?" Matt said nervously. "Kris, you're not thinking of leaving Raintree and joining the competition, are you?"

Kris winced. Even though she could tell Matt had been trying to turn his question into a joke, it had fallen pretty flat.

"No way, dude," Melina told Matt with a wink. "She's much more use to us as a spy working on the inside. She already told us all your training secrets. I was planning to torture your feeding plan out of her next."

For a moment, Matt looked flustered, but then he relaxed into a smile. "Okay, whatever," he said. "It's just that I didn't realize Kris knew anyone around here except us and the Davises," he explained. "It took me by surprise to see her hanging out with someone from another barn."

"Yeah, well, Kris and I are like the United Nations of horse racing," Melina said. "We'll probably burst into a spontaneous round of 'Kumbaya' any second now."

"Funny." Matt rolled his eyes, clearly trying to hold back a smile. "So, Kris, you ready to hit the road?"

"Yeah, I'm coming." Kris shot Melina an apologetic glance. "Sorry to cut out on you in the middle of this." She waved a hand toward the half-finished bandaging job.

"No problem. This little lady ground-ties better than most of the lead ponies. Besides, this way I won't feel guilty for not sharing my paycheck." Melina grinned at her. "Seriously, though, it's been fun. Stop by the next time you're at the track, okay? It's always a challenge finding cool people to hang with around here."

"Sure." Kris tried to keep the excitement out of her voice. Cool? Stop by next time? She had been totally hoping Melina would suggest that. There was no way she'd miss all the action . . . or the new friend.

So far, the only real friends near her age

she'd made since coming to Raintree were Matt and his best friend, Junior Davis, who lived on a neighboring ranch. But the fact that Junior was one of the best-looking guys Kris had ever met—as well as one of the biggest flirts—didn't make deep friendship all that realistic. Meanwhile, the only other person she knew was Junior's sister, Dani. And she and her rich, snobby friends seemed to regard Kris as an annoying interloper, if not a total loser.

But who needs Dani Davis and her lame friends? Kris thought as she followed Matt down the aisle toward the parking lot. I'd much rather fit in with Melina and the rest of the people here at the track.

A few hours later, Kris was back at Raintree. As she was returning from checking the water in the rear broodmare pasture, she spotted Pablo at the fence line of the large weanling pasture. He was standing so still that she stopped to watch, worried that one of the youngsters might be in trouble. But Pablo didn't seem to be looking in the direction of the grazing weanlings or the swaybacked elderly gelding who served as their babysitter and companion. Instead, he was peering down at the fence in front of him.

Curious, Kris hurried over. "What are you doing?" she asked.

Pablo glanced up at her. "Someone's been chewing the fence," he said, pointing to the top board.

"That's weird." Kris leaned in for a better look. Sure enough, she could see rough gouges in several spots in the wood. She looked out toward the weanlings. "I didn't know any of the weaners were wood chewers."

"I didn't, either." Pablo rubbed his chin and squinted out at the horses.

One of the weanlings suddenly noticed the humans standing there. Letting out a squeal, the young horse kicked up his heels and then trotted toward them. Soon the rest of the little herd was following.

Kris smiled as she watched the weanlings frolic their way over to the fence. Right behind them came the babysitter horse, a twenty-something retired racehorse and lead pony

known as Gent because of his kind tempera-
ment and good manners.

"Hi, babies," Kris cooed as the horses
reached the fence. She reached over to offer
pats to the eager babies, reserving a few special
scratches for Gent when he made his way to
her through the wriggly mass of younger
horses. "How you doing, old fella?"

Glancing over at Pablo, she saw him staring
thoughtfully at Gent.

"I wonder if he could be behind this fence
damage," Pablo said, speaking more to himself than to Kris. "Gent *is* a cribber."

Kris frowned. Cribbing was a nasty stable
vice in which a horse repeatedly grabbed on to
a solid object with its teeth, then arched its
neck and sucked in a big gulp of air. Even
though most cribbers didn't actually chew on
the fences, stall walls, or other objects they
used to anchor themselves, the effect was
often almost the same.

"No way!" Kris said, giving Gent another
pat. "I've never seen him crib on anything out
here—only when he has to stay in a stall."

"That's true." Pablo was still staring at

Gent. "I just hope he hasn't decided to branch out to cribbing when he's turned out, too. It's not a big deal if he cribs a little inside, since he's hardly ever stalled. But if he's started doing it out here . . ."

Shaking his head, Pablo glanced down at his watch. Then he said a quick good-bye to Kris and walked off in the direction of the barn.

Kris watched him go, her good mood suddenly flagging slightly. Pablo seems really bothered, she thought, reaching up to scratch Gent around the base of his ears. The old gelding tilted his head, his lower lip flapping with pleasure and his eyes half-closed. But he wouldn't get rid of a sweet horse like Gent for something as minor as a few fence boards . . . would he?

Biting her lip, she stared at Gent's contented face. It was no secret that Raintree wasn't in the best financial shape these days. There was not much extra money lying around to replace damaged fence boards *or* replace a group of cribbing weanlings. She hated to think Pablo might be forced to do something drastic.

Suddenly, one of the weanlings spooked playfully at a bird flying past it, and within seconds the whole herd was in motion, running joyously across the broad, grassy pasture. Gent let out a snort and took off after them, his slow but long canter stride still showing hints of the racehorse he had once been. Kris shaded her eyes as she watched him catch up.

"Go, Gent!' she said aloud with a smile. Seeing the herd kick up their heels had chased away her worries as quickly as they'd come.

It probably wasn't Gent chewing the fence, anyway, she reminded herself. If he's never cribbed in turnout before, why would he start now?

Chapter Three

"Hi there, gorgeous."

Kris jumped, both at the voice in her ear and the hands that had suddenly squeezed her waist. Blushing furiously, she spun around, almost knocking over the wheelbarrow she'd just filled with manure and soiled bedding. "Junior!" she cried, pushing away the grinning guy standing there. "You shouldn't sneak up on people like that—especially people holding sharp, pointy objects." She held up her pitchfork in mock warning.

Junior Davis kept grinning. "Sorry. I just can't resist a woman with horse poop on her elbow."

"Whatever." Tucking her hair behind her ear, Kris hid a smile as she pushed the wheelbarrow into the barn aisle, pretending she was going to roll it right over the toe of Junior's expensive loafer. It had been a few days since Kris had been to the track, and she had to admit it was nice to see someone besides Pablo or Matt. Especially someone as easy on the eyes as Junior. With his classic good looks and charming personality, he had the unnerving ability to brighten anybody's day—even if they didn't necessarily want that to happen. "So what are you doing here?" she asked, jumping back into the here and now. "Besides bothering me, I mean."

"We were just on our way to the track to see one of Dad's horses run, and we stopped by to see if Matt wanted to join us." Junior's playful eyes lit up. "Hey! I have a great idea. Why don't you come along, too? The more the merrier."

"We?" Kris repeated. "Who's 'we'?"

Before Junior could respond, an impatient female voice called out his name. A second later, his sister, Dani, strode around the corner into the stable aisle, followed closely by her best friend, Amber.

"Did you find Matt, or what?" Dani asked her brother. Then, spotting Kris standing with Junior, she stopped short and frowned. "Oh. Hello."

"Hi." Kris smiled tightly. It was a huge understatement to say that she and Dani didn't get along. They had a *lot* of issues. For one thing, Dani and Matt Ritter had been an item for as long as anyone could remember, but once Kris had come on the scene he'd seemed to forget Dani had ever meant anything to him. Dani made no secret of the fact that she still held a grudge about that. And it didn't help that Junior flirted with Kris constantly. Dani made it *very* clear that she thought both Matt and Junior were too good for someone like Kris. They had grown up with all the advantages that had been lacking on the streets of Oakland, and Dani tried never to let Kris forget it.

Then there was Amber. Kris often wished she and Dani could start over and figure out a way to be friends. But Amber? She wished that girl would just go away. Not only was Amber as snobby as Dani, she was also one of the most boring people Kris had ever met.

As if reading Kris's thoughts, Amber let one slender hand drift lazily through her long, straight blond hair and asked, "Why are you standing around here doing nothing, Junior?" Her voice, as always, hovered dangerously close to a petulant whine. "I thought we needed to hurry to get over to the track in time to see your stupid race."

"Yeah," Dani said, crossing her arms over her chest. "Let's find Matt and get going already."

"Kris is going to come along, too," Junior told her. "Isn't that right, Kris?"

Kris hesitated. Normally she would have brushed aside Junior's flirtatious invitation and said no without a second thought. Being stuck in a car with Dani and Amber wasn't her idea of a fun day out. But her last visit to the track had been so great. Melina and the rest of the crew had made her feel more welcome in an hour or two than Dani and Amber had in the whole time she had been at Raintree.

Plus, I miss seeing Wildfire around this

place, Kris thought, her gaze drifting down the aisle to his empty stall. It would be nice to visit him today.

"I guess a trip to the track could be fun," she told Junior. "I'll have to ask Pablo if I can knock off a little early, though."

Amber frowned. "How are we supposed to fit five people in your tiny Porsche?" she asked Junior.

"Amber's right," Dani said. Shooting Kris a sickly-sweet fake smile, she added, "Sorry, Kris. Maybe next time."

"Don't be ridiculous, sis," Junior said breezily. "I'm sure you can all squeeze in." He waggled his eyebrows. "If you run out of room back there, Kris can always ride on my lap."

Kris rolled her eyes. "Very funny," she said. "I'll go find Pablo."

It didn't take her long to track down the trainer. He was standing beside the fence of the weanling pasture, at the same spot where she'd found him before. A few yards away, Gent and his young charges were nosing at a pile of hay.

"Damage is getting worse," Pablo said as Kris skidded to a stop in front of him. He reached out and ran his calloused fingers over the damaged wood. "Whoever's chewing on it is really doing a number on it."

"Bummer," Kris said absently. She was too rushed to worry about wood-chewing at the moment. "Listen, Pablo. Junior and Matt are going to the track right now, and they invited me along. I just finished doing stalls, grain is mixed for tonight, and everyone's turned out with plenty of hay and water. All I have left to do today is unpack that new shipment of supplements that just came in, and I can do that when I get back."

"Hmm." Pablo was still staring at the fence.

Kris waited another few seconds, but he didn't say anything else. She wasn't sure he'd even been listening to her.

"So how about it?" she prompted, wondering if she was going to have to explain the whole thing again. "Can I go?"

He finally glanced up at her. "What? Oh, sure, no problem. Go ahead."

"Thanks!" Kris smiled. "I'll work extra-hard

tomorrow, I swear. Oh! And I'll tell Wildfire you said hi."

"Sounds good." Pablo smiled briefly in return, but his gaze had already wandered back to the damaged boards and the horses in the pasture beyond. "This isn't good," he muttered, obviously talking to himself now rather than to Kris. "If this doesn't stop, it might be time to get some juice out here. . . ."

Kris froze, wondering if she'd heard him right. The local equine vet often referred to the "blue juice" he used to euthanize horses. Could that really be what Pablo was talking about?

No way! she thought, her brain throbbing with shock. That's crazy—Pablo wouldn't put down a sweet horse like Gent just for chewing up a couple of boards . . . would he?

She opened her mouth to ask. But before she could say anything, Pablo hurried off toward the barn. Kris took a few steps after him, but then she heard a shout from the other direction. Glancing over her shoulder, she saw Junior and Matt waving to her from the Porsche. She hesitated, looking from the two guys back to Gent and the weanlings.

Oh, well, she told herself. It's not like he's going to rush out and put Gent down right this minute. I can talk to him about it when I get back from the track.

"Coming!" she called to the guys, giving them a wave as she turned and hurried toward the car.

The ride to the track in the cramped car was uncomfortable, both physically *and* mentally. Her decision to come along had been made on impulse, but once she had the chance to think it over she wondered if she might be reading too much into Melina's friendliness the other day. Just because they'd spent a couple of hours hanging out didn't necessarily mean Melina wanted to be Kris's new best friend. . . .

But her worries were put to rest as soon as she reached the Trenton Stables area. As she turned the corner at the end of the main shedrow, she spotted Mac Mackenzie walking a horse down the aisle. He spotted her, too, and gave her a friendly wave.

"Yo, it's Mel's friend. Kris, right?" the exercise rider said. "We met the other day."

"Yeah, I remember," Kris said. "How's it going?"

Mac patted the horse he was leading. "Still trying to stay on top," he said with a wink.

Kris grinned. "Glad to hear it. Um, I was looking for Melina. Is she around?"

"That way." Mac gestured down the aisle. "She's in the tack stall—last one on the right."

"Thanks." As Mac moved on with his charge, Kris walked down the aisle, pausing briefly to give Beau a pat as she passed his stall.

When she reached the tack stall, she spotted Melina inside, sitting on an upturned bucket with a mass of leather straps on her lap and a bar of saddle soap balanced on one knee. Standing nearby was a young man around Melina's age with wavy blond hair, green eyes, and a boyishly handsome face. He was chatting with Melina while he cleaned a saddle perched on the wooden rack in front of him. Kris couldn't help taking a surprised breath.

The guy was hot! Where was he the other day? she thought. And why did I not stop and change before I came out here?

At the sound of Kris's gasp, they both looked up. "Kris!" Melina cried happily. "Hi! What are you doing here? There aren't any Raintree horses running today, are there?"

"Nope." Kris stepped over the threshold, taking a deep breath of the musky scent of good leather, oil, and saddle soap and avoiding eye contact with the hottie. Please don't be blushing, she begged herself silently as out loud she explained, "I rode over with Junior Davis—he's my neighbor. His dad has one going today."

"Cool." Melina smiled, then gestured to her companion. "By the way, this is Logan. I don't think you met him the other day."

"No, she didn't," Logan said immediately, setting down his tack sponge and wiping both hands on his jeans before stepping forward to offer one to Kris. When he smiled, his teeth looked superwhite in his tanned face, their gleam almost rivaling that of the thick gold watch he wore on his left wrist. "I would definitely remember if we'd met," he added. "Definitely."

"I'm Kris Furillo." Kris shook his hand. "Nice to meet you," she added.

"Likewise." Logan gave her hand one last squeeze before letting it go. "So what's your story, Kris?"

"Don't you recognize her, dummy?" Melina said. "Kris is the one who rescued that horse Wildfire a while back. Remember? It was all over the TV when it happened."

"That was you?" Logan looked impressed. "Wow, beautiful *and* brave. So what are you doing hanging around with a couple of losers like us? You should be off giving interviews to *People* magazine or something."

Kris shrugged, feeling a little embarrassed even though it was obvious he was just kidding around. Deciding it might be wise to change the subject before she turned apple colored, she glanced around the small tack room. It was jammed full of saddles, bridles and bits of all types, extra stirrup leathers, girths, martingales, and countless other pieces of leather and racing equipment.

"So, you guys are cleaning tack, huh?" she said. "You're in luck. I happen to be an expert tack cleaner myself. Need some help?"

"Always," Melina said promptly. Then she blinked, suddenly looking worried. "By the way, Kris, I hope you don't think I only like to hang out with you because you help me with my job. I'd still be happy to see you even if you just followed me around with your hands in your pockets, like some of the useless owners that stop by sometimes."

Logan grinned. "You feel the same way about me, right, Mel?"

Melina snorted. "Oh, yeah, the exact same way. The only difference is, you *never* do anything useful around here."

Kris smiled and grabbed another empty bucket to use as a seat, amazed by how much she already felt at home with Melina and the other racetrack workers.

As Melina and Logan continued to trade playful barbs, Kris observed. Clearly, Melina and Logan had been working together for a while. They had the whole brother/sister vibe going, which, Kris had to admit, she was pretty happy about. The last thing she wanted to do was go and get a crush on her new friend's guy.

Grabbing a bridle out of the pile on the floor nearby, she started taking it apart, her fingers automatically unbuckling the noseband and detaching the reins from the bit. I guess I sort of assumed, Kris thought, I'd just have to put up with a bunch of snotty rich people like Dani Davis and her friends if I wanted to be part of the racing world, or, at best, the nicer ones like the Ritters, who still can't possibly understand where I'm coming from half the time, no matter how hard they try.

She laughed and ducked out of the way as Melina threw a dirty saddle sponge at Logan for something he'd just said. Clearly, the pair never stopped teasing. Kris felt herself relax even more. It looked like the racing world had some normal people in it, after all.

"So, Kris," Logan said casually, interrupting her thoughts. "Does your boyfriend ever come to the track with you?"

"Subtle, dude," Melina said, chucking yet another sponge in his direction.

"Whoever said I claimed to be subtle? I'm just asking the lady a question."

Kris blushed, then bent lower over the girth she was now cleaning to hide her reaction. "I'm not really seeing anybody right now," she said. "I'm still kind of new around here."

"Oh, dear," Logan said cheerfully. "We'll have to try to fix that, won't we?"

"Lay off, Hormone Boy," Melina told him with mock sternness. "I don't want you scaring Kris away."

"She doesn't look like the type who scares easily." Logan winked at Kris, then hoisted the now-clean saddle off the rack in front of him and turned to set it back on one of the metal racks on the wall.

Kris laughed. "You're right," she told Logan playfully. "I ride thousand-pound animals for a living, not to mention shoveling thousands of pounds of their poop every day. 'Scared' doesn't really fit in my vocabulary."

Melina giggled, and Logan looked amused. "You and me both," he said, grabbing another saddle. "If my parents threatening to disown me couldn't scare me, nothing will." At Kris's confused look, he added, "They were after me to go to Harvard Business School like my brother instead of coming to work at the track."

"Harvard Business School?" Kris said. "Wow, you must be pretty smart if they wanted you to go there."

"No way," Melina put in mischievously. "When Harvard has a building named after your granddad, you don't have to be smart to get in."

Before she could say another word, Logan grabbed the tack sponge Melina had thrown at him and winged it back at her head. But he was grinning. "Shut up, Mel," he said. "You're making me look *ad-bay* in front of the *abe-bay*."

Kris smiled distractedly, recognizing that she should be flattered by what he'd just said, not upset. But something felt off. As the gold watch on Logan's arm caught the overhead light again, she focused on it, realizing that what she'd thought was a Rolex knockoff was probably the real thing.

Maybe I was wrong, she thought with a

pang of disappointment. Maybe I haven't found people who are exactly "normal," after all.

But, as Melina and Logan continued to chat and joke around, Kris gradually found herself forgetting Logan's status. Whatever his background, he was one of the nicest, most likable people she'd ever met. He seemed ready to accept Kris at face value, so she figured she might as well try to return the favor. And even better, he was the complete opposite of Dani and her friends. If he had money, at least he didn't find it necessary to flaunt it.

"Logan! There you are. I've been looking everywhere for you."

Kris glanced up as a harsh voice filled the stall. Parker, the assistant trainer she'd met the other day, was standing in the doorway with a slight frown on his delicate face.

"Hi, Parker!" Melina said, her eyes lighting up. "What's up?"

Parker shot her a brief smile, then spotted Kris. "Oh, it's you," he said. "The girl from Raintree. What are you doing in here?"

"She's stealing all our training secrets," Logan replied with a straight face. "The Ritters are watching this very conversation through a two-way camera hidden in her belt buckle."

Melina laughed, but Parker did not seem amused. "Logan, I need you to come help Shawn out with that big new filly," he said. "She's obviously never had her feet done properly before, and she's putting up a fuss."

"No problem, boss. I'll be right there." Logan set down his sponge and capped the leather conditioner he'd been using. Parker had already disappeared again, and after a glance at the doorway, Logan shot Kris a smile. "So I guess you already know Parker," he said. "Don't take anything he says too seriously. As you may have noticed, he's a little uptight."

"No, he's not," Melina said quickly. "He's got a lot of responsibility here, and he takes it really seriously. Nothing wrong with that." She smiled at Kris. "Parker's cool—you just need to get to know him better. He used to be a pretty successful jockey before he got into training."

"Yeah!" Logan added in a high-pitched, goofy voice. "And his blue eyes are *soooo* dreamy!" He laughed as Melina scowled at him, then added in his normal voice, "See you guys later."

"Bye," Kris said. And, as he disappeared through the doorway, Kris realized . . . she was sorry to see him go.

Chapter Four

"Don't pay any attention to Logan's goofing around," Melina said when the two of them were alone. "He makes fun of everything. Parker's cool, seriously."

"He seems really capable," Kris responded. She was also tempted to say something about Melina's obvious crush on the assistant trainer, but she decided to keep quiet. If Melina hadn't brought it up herself, maybe there was a reason. But just because Melina is avoiding the boy topic, doesn't mean *I* have to, too, Kris thought with a smile. "Um, so Logan seems nice," she added out loud.

"Do I detect a hint of interest there, Ms. Furillo?" Melina asked with a laugh. "But yeah,

Logan's great. A little nuts, maybe, but great. I mean, he has to be a little unwell to get up at the butt crack of dawn every day to cater to a bunch of four-legged manure machines when he could be living off his trust fund down in Cabo."

"So he really does come from money, huh?" Kris did her best to keep her voice casual as she scrubbed at a spot on the leather in her hand.

"Oh, yeah. His family's loaded."

Kris bit her lip as another question came to her. Melina seemed awfully matter-of-fact about Logan's background. What if she came from money, too? All this time Kris had been assuming that her new friend's well-worn jeans and down-to-earth attitude meant she was just like her. But maybe not.

"He's not stuck up about it, though," Melina went on, oblivious to Kris's inner turmoil. "He treats everyone the same, whether they're poor or rich." She winked. "Unlike most people at the track."

Kris smiled ruefully. "Yeah, tell me about it," she said. "Sometimes I feel like people look at me as some kind of freak show just because I have to work for every penny."

"Oh, I hear you! I'm pretty used to that feeling myself," Melina replied. "Growing up with seven brothers and sisters and never enough money for luxuries like shoes that actually fit, I always got plenty of those pitying looks from the Richie Riches of the world."

Kris relaxed. So Melina wasn't an undercover rich girl, after all! Even though she knew it shouldn't matter, she couldn't help being relieved. It felt more comfortable to be on the same footing.

"Wow! Seven brothers and sisters?" Kris said, trying to imagine it. "That must have been wild."

Melina chuckled and reached down to fish another dirty stirrup leather out of the pile on the floor. "Sometimes," she said. "That's how I got into horses. Coming to the track was my escape from the craziness at home. My folks weren't thrilled at first, though. I was kind of a wild and crazy kid anyway—you know, mouthing off to teachers, smoking out behind the school, the whole deal—and they thought I might run into too many bad influences hanging around the racetrack."

Kris rolled her eyes. "Bad influences, here?" she said. "Compared to my life before, hanging out at the track is like Sunday school for me. . . ." Somehow, she found herself telling Melina all about the tough crowd in her old neighborhood and the car theft that had landed her at Camp LaGrange.

"Whoa," she said when Kris finished. "Good for you for finding your way out of that mess. See, I knew you were cool when I met you!"

Kris smiled, relieved that Melina didn't seem to be judging her too harshly for her troubled past. She'd shared her story on impulse, and for a second, she'd wondered if that had been a mistake. "I'm definitely trying to make my life here work," Kris said. "I don't want to go back to where I was. . . ."

Suddenly, Melina glanced down at her watch. "Hey, I don't want to cut your story short, but it's almost time for the fourth race," she said. "A friend of mine is riding the favorite—I already planned my lunch break so I could go watch. Want to come?"

"Sure!" Kris said, falling in step as Melina

led the way through the crowds to the grand-stand.

A few minutes later they arrived at the apron and, finding a free spot at the rail near the finish line, they leaned forward in anticipation. Soon the horses stepped onto the track for the post parade.

Kris felt a familiar thrill run through her as the track announcer started listing the entrants for the race. She loved this moment. Even when Wildfire wasn't running, she loved being at the track, watching the beautiful, fit horses do their thing. "Which one's your friend?" she asked Melina.

"He's on the eight horse," Melina replied, pointing. "Blue-and-yellow silks." Cupping her hands around her mouth, she shouted, "Yo, *amigo*! You learn to ride yet?"

The jockey on the number eight horse heard her and glanced over, grinning. He reached down to pat his mount, an athletic-looking bay gelding with a crooked blaze, then tossed Melina a quick salute.

Melina waved back, then turned to Kris. "That's Carlos," she said. "He's a doll. I've known him since I was, like, thirteen. He was pretty much my volunteer babysitter back when I was an impressionable youth and he was a lowly exercise rider. Now he's one of the top-winning jocks at this track."

"I recognize him," Kris said, peering at the jockey's face beneath the blue-and-yellow helmet. "I think he's ridden for the Ritters once or twice."

"Yeah. He rides for most of the top barns around here."

The two of them continued to chat about Carlos, his mount, and the other horses in the race as they watched the field make its way to the starting gate. Most of the horses loaded easily, including Carlos's. But the last horse in line balked in front of the gate, tossing his head and backing up.

"Uh-oh," Kris said, quickly flashing to Wildfire's trouble with the starting gate. "I hope he doesn't hold up the race."

Melina was peering at the big screen in the middle of the infield, which was showing a close-up view of the problem horse. "Don't worry," she said confidently. "That's just Bold

Timbre. He does this before almost every race. Zane will get him in."

"Zane?" Kris said. "Is that Bold Timbre's jockey?"

Melina shook her head. "Assistant starter," she said. "He's that big Mack truck of a guy coming over to the horse now." She pointed to a burly figure on the screen. As they watched, the man locked hands with another assistant starter and physically pushed the horse forward toward the gate. "They know this horse; all he needs is a little strong encouragement and he'll go right in."

Sure enough, a moment later Bold Timbre was standing in the gate with the others. Kris barely had time to glance over at Melina, impressed with her knowledge of everybody and everything at the track, before the bell rang and the gates sprang open.

"They're off!" the track announcer cried.

Gripping the rail in front of her, Kris leaned forward as the horses surged down the backstretch. Bold Timbre broke fast, scooting over to the rail to take the lead.

"Where's Carlos's horse?" Kris asked,

peering helplessly at the mass of horseflesh bunched behind the leader.

"Don't look for him in front yet," Melina said, raising her voice to be heard above the cheers and whistles of the crowd and the crackle of the PA system. "His horse likes to lay off the pace, but he's got one heck of a kick. He'll be there at the end, trust me."

Once again, Melina's prediction proved correct. In the last two furlongs of the race, Carlos's mount put on a burst of extra speed, quickly overtaking the leaders. By the time he swept under the finish wire, he was three lengths in front.

"Go, Carlos!" Melina whooped, pumping her fist in the air. "You got it done, baby!"

Kris grinned. Melina's enthusiasm was infectious. "That was awesome!" she cried.

Melina grabbed her arm. "Come on," she said. "Let's go get our picture taken." At Kris's confused look, she added, "In the winner's circle."

"What?" Kris was startled. "We can't do that—can we?"

"Sure, why not?" Melina shrugged. "The

owners of that horse don't even live in the state. He could use our support."

Kris giggled. "Why does it feel like we're doing something forbidden?" she wondered aloud as she followed Melina across the apron toward the low wall enclosing the winner's circle.

Melina winked at her over her shoulder. "Hey, it's not grand theft auto," she quipped. "But it'll have to do for now."

Kris rolled her eyes. "Very funny." Even though the joke was at her expense, she didn't mind. Coming from Melina, it just felt like normal banter. Now, if Dani had said something like that . . . Kris thought. But before she could go down that road, they reached the winner's circle.

"Coming through, coming through," Melina said loudly. "We're with the winner."

The track worker inside raised an eyebrow as they entered. "Hi, Melina," he said. "So you're part-owner of this one, too, eh?"

"You got it, Mikey." Melina grinned at the young man. "This is Kris. She's a part-owner, too."

Mikey rolled his eyes, but waved them through. A moment later Carlos arrived, still in the saddle.

The jockey's face was coated with track dirt except around his eyes, which had been protected by goggles during the race. "Ah, here's little Melinamina," he said in a voice that was surprisingly deep and husky for his small frame. "So it worked—you were my good-luck charm today."

"Always," Melina replied. "Hey, Carlos, this is Kris Furillo. She's the one who . . ."

But Kris didn't hear the rest of Melina's explanation. She had just spotted Matt, Junior, Dani, and Amber standing outside the winner's circle looking in . . . right at her. Junior looked amused, Matt looked a little perplexed, and both girls looked downright annoyed.

Oops, she thought. I've been having so much fun with Melina that I completely forgot that the others were still at the track. Guess I'm busted. . . .

She turned back just in time to see Carlos lean down and offer his hand. Stepping forward, she took it. "Nice to meet you," she said.

"That was some great riding you did out there."

"Thanks, Miss Furillo," Carlos said. "I hear you're becoming quite a rider yourself. Maybe we'll ride against each other someday soon, eh?"

Kris was still blushing at Carlos's comment when the track photographer snapped a picture of the whole group. Then Carlos swung down from the saddle and hurried toward the scales to weigh out while a groom led the tired horse away.

As Kris and Melina wandered out of the winner's circle, Junior and the others came over. Preparing to be mocked, Kris forced a smile on her face.

"Nice work, Kris," Junior said with a wink. "Sneaking yourself into a win picture—well done."

"Yeah," Dani said drily. "I'm sure the horse's owners will be just thrilled to get a photo of some total stranger standing next to their horse with a goofy grin on her face."

Kris hadn't really thought about that, but she shrugged it off. If the owners didn't even live in the state, they probably had no idea what their horse's grooms looked like. Besides, she was sure Dani was just trying to get under her skin, as usual.

"Guys, this is Melina," she said without bothering to respond to the barb. "She works for Jeff Trenton." She quickly introduced Junior, Dani, and Amber.

Junior looked impressed. "Trenton Stables, huh?" he said as he shook Melina's hand. "That's a pretty good outfit."

"Only *pretty* good?" Melina teased. "I guess we can't all be *really* good like Davis Farms, huh?"

Junior raised an eyebrow in surprise, but Kris laughed. "Don't pay any attention to her," she advised him. "She gives everybody a hard time." She smiled at Matt, who was nodding his agreement.

"She does, huh?" Junior held on to Melina's hand, a flirtatious smile playing around his lips as he took in her slim yet curvy figure. "Maybe that's because she hasn't met anyone who can keep up with her yet."

Dani rolled her eyes. "Relax, Junior," she

said bitingly. "Your other working-class lust object is standing right there, remember?"

Amber giggled, Junior rolled his eyes, and Matt looked as if he suddenly wished he were somewhere else. Frowning, Kris clenched her fists at her sides. It was certainly no secret that she and Junior had a little flirtation going, and it was hardly the first time Dani had openly sneered at Kris's lowly roots. But this was beyond the usual attitude. She'd just met Melina. There was no need to be *so* rude.

Even Melina looked surprised as she glanced over uncertainly at Dani. Watching them eye one another, Kris couldn't help comparing them. As always, Dani's hair and makeup were impeccable. Her artfully tousled dark waves were swept back from her face just enough to reveal the diamond studs in her ears, and her full lips were lined with a muted shade of red that perfectly complemented the lining of her designer jacket.

Melina, on the other hand, looked exactly like what she was—a hardworking groom. Her Wranglers and T-shirt looked dirty and well worn, bits of hay were in her reddish hair, and there was not a spot of makeup on her freckled face.

I guess it's not too hard to tell the haves from the have-nots at the track, Kris thought ruefully. Well, except for a few exceptions like Logan . . .

As if on cue, Logan himself suddenly emerged from the track building. "Mel!" he called, waving as he spotted them. "There you are. Did you see your boy Carlos tear up the track just now?"

Amber blinked slowly as Logan came toward them. "Who," she announced, "is *that*?"

"Yum," Dani said in a voice just loud enough for Amber—and Kris, who happened to be standing close—to hear. "And here I thought this day at the track was going to be boring."

By then, Logan had reached their little group. Melina and Kris introduced him to the others. "So you're a groom, huh?" Amber said, fluttering her long lashes at Logan. "That's hot. Right, Dani?"

"Definitely," Dani said, sidling a little closer

to Logan. "It takes a real man to deal with race-horses all day long."

"Hear that, Kris?" Melina said. "You and I must be real men."

Kris grinned while Dani shot Melina an irritated glance before quickly arranging her face into a slightly fake-looking smile. "Good one, Melinda," she said. "You're funny."

What's funny, actually, Kris thought, is just how friendly Dani got as soon as a cute guy appeared. Kris noticed Melina shooting her a smirk. Clearly, she's thinking the same thing. I should have known Melina would figure out what Dani's about right away.

"It's Melina," Melina corrected, returning her gaze to Dani. Then she glanced at her watch and let out a gasp. "Yo, I've got to scoot! Rosie's getting picked up in, like, twenty minutes, and I still need to get her ready."

"Rosie?" Amber repeated, wrinkling her nose. "Who's that? Do you have a kid or something?"

"Technicolor Rose," Logan answered for Melina. "She's a horse. Mel's her groom."

Melina nodded. "And Parker's going to kill

me if she's not wrapped and ready when the van shows up," she said. "She's supposed to ship out to another track today."

"I'll help you get her ready," Kris offered. "Come on, if we hurry, Parker won't even need to know you were late."

"I'll help, too," Logan added. "I'm still technically on my lunch break, so I've got nothing better to do."

Dani stepped closer and put a hand on his arm. "I'm *sure* we could find you something better to do if we try hard," she said, tilting her head and giving him a little half-smile. "Those two can handle that horse without you, can't they?"

Logan smiled back, but shook his head firmly. "I'd better take a rain check on that, Dani," he said. "See you around."

He fell into step beside Melina and Kris as they hurried toward the path to the backside. Kris glanced back and smiled. As she had expected, there was a *very* disgruntled expression on Dani's face.

Poor Dani, she thought, amused. She's used to getting whatever she wants whenever she wants it. Too bad Logan didn't read the memo.

But a moment later, when they rounded the corner into the shedrow, the smile vanished from Kris's face. It looked like utter chaos. People were shouting and running this way and that, while horses stamped their feet in their stalls and let out loud whinnies.

"What's happening?" Kris exclaimed.

Logan's eyes widened, and he pointed toward the far end of the row. "Loose horse!"

Following his gaze, Kris saw a light chestnut with long, white stockings rear up in the middle of the aisle.

Melina gasped. "Rosie!" she cried.

Chapter Five

From where she stood, Kris saw that José, the gruff older groom she'd met on her previous visit, was standing right in front of the chestnut filly. He was speaking soothingly to her in Spanish, but Rosie was rolling her eyes and dancing in place, not interested in paying attention. When José took a cautious step toward her, she wheeled and clattered off down the aisle at a brisk trot.

"Somebody head her off!" Parker cried. He was standing nearby, holding a lead shank in one hand. Mac Mackenzie jumped forward to try to grab the filly as she passed him, but Rosie easily dodged him and kept going.

"Rosie!" Melina cried, leaping forward. "Whoa, girl!"

Kris was staring at the excited filly, wondering what to do, when Logan grabbed her hand. "Let's go this way," he said, gesturing back toward the corner.

She nodded, instantly understanding his thinking. If they could dash around through the next shedrow, they might be able to cut Rosie off before she could escape from the aisle. Then somebody would be able to come from behind and catch her.

They rounded the corner together, then burst into a run, ignoring the surprised looks from the grooms in the next aisle. Kris slowed her pace before making the corner, not wanting to startle the filly, who was already pretty worked up.

It was a good thing she did, as she almost crashed into Shorty. He was standing still, watching the filly come toward them. Rosie had slowed from a trot to a prancy walk and was now swinging her head back and forth, looking at the horses in their stalls as she passed.

Shorty glanced at Kris and Logan. "Oh, good," he said in his usual slow, relaxed voice. "Reinforcements."

"Let's spread out and head her off," Logan said. "I doubt she actually wants to go anywhere—looks like she's just enjoying some sightseeing at this point."

Sure enough, once the filly saw the three humans moving toward her, she quickly gave up and allowed herself to be captured. As Shorty led her back down the aisle, Melina reached them.

"Rosie, you about gave me a heart attack!" she scolded the horse fondly, giving her a pat. "I thought we were over the escape-artist shtick, girly."

Parker hurried up and snapped his lead rope onto the filly's halter. "I thought we were over that, too," he said, his voice tight and angry. "Someone must have left her stall door unlatched."

"It wasn't me, I swear!" Melina said quickly. "I double-checked it last time I was in there, just like always." She glanced at Kris. "Rosie's an equine Houdini. You have to latch her stall door at the bottom. If you just do it at the top, like with most of the horses, she lets herself out."

"Well, nobody else has been in that filly's stall all afternoon," Parker said icily. "Are you suggesting that we have a poltergeist, Melina?"

Melina's face flushed bright red and Kris bit her lip, feeling sorry for her friend. It was no fun to get yelled at, especially when you weren't at fault. And having it come from the guy you were crushing on? That only made it worse.

"Take it easy, Parker," Logan said quietly. "You know Mel doesn't make stupid mistakes like that." His gaze fell on Kris, and he grinned. "It was probably our little spy here," he added jokingly, jerking a thumb in Kris's direction. "Everyone knows she's just hanging around here trying to sabotage us on behalf of the Ritters."

The barn aisle had been so silent you could hear a horseshoe nail drop, but at Logan's comment there was a burst of laughter, and the tension level immediately dropped. Kris smiled, too, but she felt uneasy—especially when she noticed that Parker was just about the only one *not* laughing.

The only other person not laughing was Melina, though she appeared to be doing her best to smile. "Um, so is the van here yet?" she asked Parker. "I still need to get Rosie wrapped. . . ."

"Forget that," Parker snapped, turning his attention back to Melina. "I'm not sending her in this state." He nodded toward the filly, who was breathing hard, sweat dotting her flanks. "Rub her down and put her away. I'll have to reschedule her trip for tomorrow." Without another word he strode off, muttering under his breath.

Kris walked beside Melina as she led Rosie back toward her stall. "Wow," Kris whispered. "Is he always that intense?"

Melina shrugged, looking worried and a bit crestfallen. "Parker has a lot of responsibility around here," she said. "Mr. Trenton depends on him, and he likes to run a tight ship, you know?"

The two of them didn't talk much as they

tended to the filly. But by the time Rosie was cooled off and calmly munching hay in her stall, Melina was almost back to her old self.

"Beau didn't work out today, so I told José I'd take him for a walk to stretch his legs," Melina said. "Want to help?"

"Definitely!" Kris said, eager to spend any time she could with the beautiful colt.

As they approached his stall, Beau gazed out at them with calm, liquid eyes. He greeted them with a soft nicker, then stood patiently as Melina adjusted his halter and hooked on the lead shank.

"Wow," Kris said as she watched. "If Wildfire doesn't get out in the morning, he practically runs me over to escape from his stall. We have to make sure he gets enough exercise when he's at the track without his usual turnout."

"Yeah, most of them are like that." Melina gave the horse a scratch on the neck. "But Beau's a pretty special guy."

Beau continued to demonstrate his good manners as Kris and Melina walked him down the stable aisle. They left the Trenton Stables section, heading toward the grassy area between the barns and the backside parking lot, where the grooms could take their charges to graze. As they walked along, Kris noticed people shooting the big chestnut admiring looks. She wondered if they recognized him and knew about his impressive race record, or if they were just taking the time to appreciate his big, glossy, muscular good looks and gentlemanly behavior.

"Here we go, Beau-Beau," Melina said when they reached the grazing area. There were no other horses there at the moment, so she led Beau to the middle and gave him a pat. "It's all yours."

The grass was sunbaked and sparse, but Beau lowered his head and began grazing as contentedly as if it were lush Kentucky bluegrass. Kris smiled as she watched him eat.

"He's such a cool horse," she said. "You guys are lucky to have him."

"Trust me, we know," Melina replied. "Everyone in the barn adores Beau."

Kris nodded. "It's not too often that you see the whole package like that," she mused. "He's sweet, he's fast, and he's a total knockout all at the same time."

Beau lifted his head and gazed at her as if he'd heard and understood what she'd just said. Taking a half step toward her, he nuzzled at her chest, drooling green slime down her shirt.

Kris pushed him gently away with a giggle. "Ew! Thanks a lot, Beau!" she cried. "Okay, so maybe no horse is *completely* perfect. . . ."

Except Wildfire, a little voice in her head piped up. You still think he's perfect. Don't you?

Suddenly, Kris felt a pang of guilt ripple through her. She'd been so busy hanging out with Melina that she hadn't even visited Wildfire since arriving at the track. And here she was, standing around oohing and aahing over another horse when she could be spending time with her favorite horse in the world.

Beau may be sweet, good-looking, and a track-record holder and everything, she told herself uneasily. But maybe I need to spend a little more time remembering which horse I care about the most . . . the horse who got me here.

She was just about to say good-bye to Melina and head over to Wildfire's stall, when she heard voices calling her name. Looking up, she saw Matt, Junior, Dani, and Amber hurrying toward her.

"There you are," Dani said irritably, stomping across the grass. "We were about to leave without you."

"No, we weren't," Junior said with a laugh, "unless maybe you were planning to knock me out and steal the keys."

Amber tossed her long hair over one shoulder. "Whatever," she said, sounding bored. "Now that we've found her, can we finally get out of here? I'm barely going to have time for a manicure today as it is."

"Horrors!" Matt joked, earning him a sour look from Amber.

Meanwhile, Junior had stepped over to give Beau a pat. "Nice horse," he said to Melina. "I saw him win that big-stakes race last month."

"What stakes r—Wait a sec, that's not Loyal Beau, is it?" Matt asked. "Wow, he looks a lot calmer right now than he does when he's humiliating all the other horses on the track!"

Melina giggled, looking pleased at Matt's comment. "I know," she said. "Everyone says he's way too relaxed to be a racehorse. But Beau loves to prove them all wrong."

"This is all very interesting," Dani broke in, with an expression that showed she didn't find it interesting at all. "But we really have to be—"

"Dani!" Amber interrupted, elbowing her friend in the ribs. "Check it out—hottie at ten o'clock."

Following Amber's stare, Kris saw Parker coming toward them, striding through the sunshine with a light breeze ruffling his blond hair. In that light, Kris could see why Melina was so smitten. The trainer was definitely good-looking—in a fragile sort of way.

"Well, hello there!" Amber said, sidling up to him as he joined the little group. She reached out and flicked a stray piece of hay off the collar of his navy polo shirt. "I'm Amber. Who are you?"

Parker blinked. "Uh, hi," he said, seemingly caught off guard by Amber's forwardness.

"Did you need something from *me*, Parker?" Melina asked, a sharp edge creeping into her voice. She glared at Amber, who was standing as close as possible to Parker without actually touching him.

She's probably trying to get him to look down her shirt, Kris thought, noticing that the silk shirt Amber was wearing was unbuttoned halfway down her front. That's just the kind of oh-so-subtle enticement Amber seems to think works for her.

Parker glanced at Amber uncertainly, gulped, then returned his gaze to Melina. "I just came to let you know that Technicolor Rose will be shipping out tomorrow morning at eight," he said.

"Okay. I'll have her ready." Melina was still shooting daggers at Amber.

"Parker, huh?" Amber spoke up, touching the assistant trainer on the arm. "That's a cool name."

Amber must be bored, Kris thought in annoyance. Normally she'd never even look twice at a guy who's practically the same height as she is. . . .

"Excuse me," Kris blurted out, unable to take any more of the Amber flirtfest. "I've got to go say hi to Wildfire."

"What?" Dani had been watching Amber's flirting with obvious amusement, but now she spun around to face Kris with a look of outraged disbelief. "Are you kidding me? Didn't you just hear me say we're ready to leave—now?"

"I heard you," Kris retorted evenly. "And I'm pretty sure you also heard me say I've got to go see Wildfire. I'd bet you can wait a few more minutes for your stupid manicures, or whatever."

"It's okay," Junior said. Glancing over at his sister's friend with a grin, he added, "It kind of looks like Amber's not ready to go yet, anyway."

Kris grimaced as she saw Amber giggle and give Parker's arm a squeeze. Parker's confused look had faded, and he was now smiling back at her. Typical male behavior, Kris thought. Give them enough attention and they become bumbling fools.

"I'll be back in a few minutes," Kris said.

Then shooting Melina an apologetic look she wasn't sure the girl even noticed, Kris turned and fled in the direction of Wildfire's stall.

Her worlds were colliding . . . and it was not pretty.

Chapter Six

The next morning, Kris finished her chores a little early. She was halfway to Wildfire's usual turnout paddock for a quick visit and break before she remembered he was still at the track.

Why would I bother to remember something like that? she asked herself with a twisted half-smile. After all, I barely remembered he was there when I was actually *at* the track yesterday.

When she'd finally made it to Wildfire's stall the afternoon before, he'd been so happy to see her that she'd forgotten everything else, and for a few minutes all had been well. But Dani and the others had come to drag her off far too soon, leaving Kris with the nagging feeling that she'd shortchanged Wildfire.

"Oh, well," she said aloud, looking out at the turnout paddock, which today contained one of Jean Ritter's fat, old lesson horses. "Guess I'd better find something else to do."

Looking at the lesson horse gave her an idea. There's another fat, old horse on this ranch who might need me right now, she thought. Gent. Maybe I can figure out what's really going on with that pasture fence.

Pablo hadn't said anything else about Gent's cribbing, though he had mentioned he would need to pick up new fence boards soon. That meant Kris probably had a little while to clear the old gelding's name before anything happened to him.

I must have misheard Pablo yesterday, she told herself as she hurried off down the path toward the weanling pasture. There's no way he'd put a horse down over something so ridiculous. Still, it stinks that Gent could be getting blamed for something he didn't do. Maybe if I can catch one of the babies in the act, that will clear Gent's name.

When she came within sight of the pasture, Gent and the weanlings were grazing in the middle of the field. Kris paused to watch them, admiring the idyllic sight of the horses' dark bodies against the brilliant green of the grass and the glint of the afternoon sun on their healthy coats. While she was standing there, she spotted Todd walking toward the gate from the direction of the house carrying a bag.

Gent and the weanlings saw the boy approaching, too. As if on signal, the whole herd took off across the field at a gallop, tails flagged and heads up. They all skidded to a stop near the gate and milled around, clearly eager for what came next.

Unaware that he was being watched, Todd set down the shopping bag and reached inside with both hands. The whole time he chatted to the horses in a friendly, singsong voice, though Kris wasn't close enough to make out exactly what he was saying. When Todd straightened up, Kris saw that he was holding apples.

A smile spread across her face as she noticed that the herd was now standing right at the chewed spot. "Aha," she murmured as Todd fed the apples he was holding to Gent and the pushiest of the weanlings before reaching into his bag for more. "This could explain everything."

The horses waiting their turns were snorting and kicking out at one another playfully, eager to get their treats. Taking a few steps closer, Kris watched carefully, waiting for one of them to take out that impatience on the fence board.

But none of the weanlings made a move to bite at the fence. They waited their turns, then gobbled down their apples with great gusto, slobbering juice and bits of half-chewed apple all over the fence board but never coming close to touching it with their teeth.

Kris frowned. She had been so sure she'd found the answer.

Oh, well, she thought, glancing at her watch and realizing it was almost time to start mixing the evening feed so it would be all ready later. I'll get to the bottom of this mystery even if I have to come back here day and night. I didn't catch any of the weanlings chewing the fence this time, but there's no sign that Gent has any interest in it, either. And I won't let Pablo blame him without proof.

"I can't believe it's been over a week since I've ridden him," Kris exclaimed, jamming her riding helmet on her head and giving Wildfire a pat. "I hope I remember how to do it!"

Pablo smiled. "I'm sure it'll come back to you," he said. "Now here's what I want you to do. . . ."

Kris listened carefully, nodding, as Pablo outlined that day's ride. While she may have looked calm on the outside, her insides were dancing with excitement. This would be the first time since Wildfire had moved to the track that she would be riding him in his morning workout. Even though she was his usual rider on the training track back at Raintree, this was different. It felt more real somehow. Out of the corner of her eye, she could see trainers and other spectators lined up at the rail, many of them holding stopwatches along with their cups of coffee and copies of *Daily Racing Form*.

Farther down the track, a gray colt and a chestnut gelding had just finished a gallop, while a big black-bay filly was warming up at the trot around the far turn. Just outside the gap, a patient lead pony was standing quietly while a young bay colt jumped around, crashing into the pony repeatedly and reaching over to nip him on the neck.

"Ready to go?" Pablo asked, snapping her back to reality.

Kris nodded and reached back to check the girth. "I'm ready."

Pablo gave her a leg up, and she settled into the saddle, tucking her feet into the short stirrups. Wildfire shifted his weight under her, and she smiled.

"Feel okay?" Pablo asked.

Kris picked up the reins. "Feel great." She leaned forward just long enough to give Wildfire a pat. She was on her favorite horse and on a real track. How could it *not* be great? "Come on, boy. Let's do this!"

As Wildfire swung into a vigorous canter after his brief warm-up, Kris was tempted to let him go all out as he clearly wanted to do.

She fought that urge, though, forcing herself to rate his speed exactly as Pablo had specified. She knew it was all part of the training program. If Wildfire ran his heart out every morning, he wouldn't have the energy to give his all on race day. It was important to condition him correctly so that he would peak at the right time; that was the art and science of race training.

Luckily, Wildfire didn't give her too much trouble. He seemed willing to pace himself when Kris asked, as if they had been doing this all their lives. His hooves beat out a steady tattoo against the dirt track, while his ears pricked forward and his breath came in soft grunts.

"Good boy," Kris whispered into the wind, even though she doubted the horse could hear her. "Nice and easy . . ."

By the time they slowed to a cooldown trot, Kris had a big grin plastered on her face. She wished she could ride Wildfire every day like she did when he was at Raintree. But she knew that as long as he was staying at the track, these rides would probably be occasional at best. There were plenty of exercise riders available at the track, and jockeys who might want to try him out. Plus, Kris was needed at the ranch.

Oh, well, she thought, dropping one hand to give Wildfire a much-deserved scratch on the withers. *Once in a while is better than never. And he needs to spend time here at the track if he's going to become the star he deserves to be.*

When they got back to the shedrow, Kris helped Pablo untack. "So how did he look out there?" she asked as she slung the girth over the saddle and hoisted it off Wildfire. "Because he felt really great."

"He looked good," Pablo replied, sounding distracted. "Listen, Kris, I just remembered I need to take care of some paperwork at the track office. Can you put the tack away and then keep yourself busy for an hour or so before we head home?"

"Sure." Kris smiled at the hot-walker who had just appeared to take Wildfire's lead. "Hold on a second, Eddie," she said. "He ran hard today—he deserves a little something."

Reaching into her pocket, she fished out a carrot and fed it to Wildfire. The hot-walker chuckled, then headed off down the aisle with the horse in tow. Pablo strode off in the same direction. Kris watched them go, put the tack away, and then headed over toward Melina's stalls.

When she rounded the corner into the Trenton Stables area, the first person she encountered was Parker. He was walking down the aisle with his cell phone in his hand, though he quickly tucked it in his pocket and smiled when he spotted her.

"Hi there," he said before Kris could speak. "Kris from Raintree, right? How's it going?"

"Great," Kris said, a little surprised by how much friendlier he was acting than the last couple of times she'd seen him. "I was just coming to say hi to Melina. Do you know where she is?"

Parker nodded, waving one hand down the aisle. "She's mucking stalls," he said. "I'm sure she'll be thrilled to see you turn up to help." He winked and chuckled. "Don't expect me to put you on the payroll. But feel free to use any pitchfork you like."

Kris smiled politely. "Thanks."

Wow, she thought as Parker hurried off. He's sure in a good mood today. I just hope it has nothing to do with Amber and her ridiculous flirting the other day. Because that would be way too much for me to handle right now— not to mention what it would do to Melina.

She was still contemplating those thoughts when she found Melina hauling a full wheelbarrow load of soiled shavings out of a stall. "Wow," Kris joked. "Racing sure is glamorous, huh?"

"Kris!" Melina dropped the handles of the wheelbarrow and straightened up, grinning and pushing a sweaty lock of reddish hair out of her face. "Hi! I heard you rode Wildfire this morning."

Kris was surprised. "Word travels fast."

"You know it. So how'd he go?" She hoisted the wheelbarrow again. "Walk with me while we talk, okay? I still have five more stalls to do before the horses get back from their workouts."

As they walked to the manure pile, Kris told her all about her ride. Melina listened eagerly, asking questions and making a suggestion or two.

"I love riding when I get the chance," Melina said as she dumped her load of soiled straw into the steaming manure pile. "But I don't have the guts to get on the racers. No way, no how. Guess that makes me a chicken."

"Not really," Kris said. "It probably means you have more sense than I do. Anyway, you have your own talents, right?"

"Yeah. Like shoveling poop." Melina laughed. "Come on, let's get back there and I'll show you exactly how talented I am at that!"

On the way back from the manure pile with the empty wheelbarrow, they encountered Logan. He was trying to walk a barrel-chested chestnut colt, though the horse seemed more interested in backing up and spinning around than in moving forward.

"Need any help?" Melina asked.

"Yeah," Logan replied breathlessly. "Find Shorty! He's supposed to be walking this one. He's the only one who can do anything with him." He shot Kris a smile. "Hey! Good to see you again, Kris." The chestnut dodged to one side again, nearly jerking Logan off his feet.

As Melina jumped forward to help her fellow groom, Kris spotted a familiar figure at the end of the aisle. "There's Shorty now," she said, pointing.

"Praise the Lord," Logan muttered, stepping back just in time to avoid having his foot stepped on by the excited horse. "Shorty! Get your Southern butt over here, man!"

"Sorry, Logan," Shorty said in his slow drawl, increasing his pace slightly. He took over the chestnut's lead, and the horse immediately settled. "Hi, y'all," he added to Melina and Kris.

"Hi," Kris said, trying not to laugh at the exasperated look on Logan's face as he glared at the now-calm colt.

As Shorty moved on with his charge, Logan fell into step with Kris and Melina. "So what leads you to grace us with your presence again, Kris?" he asked.

Melina let out a snort. "They teach you to

talk that way at your fancy prep school, rich boy?" she asked. "Let me translate for you, Kris. He's trying to say, what the heck are you doing back here?"

Kris explained about Wildfire's workout. "I only wish I could exercise him all the time like I used to," she said, finishing with a sigh. "I miss him."

Melina smiled sympathetically, and Logan nodded. "Hey, I have an idea for something to take your mind off all that," he said as they drifted to a stop in front of an empty stall. "Come to my party tonight."

"You're having a party?" Kris asked.

Dropping the wheelbarrow handles, Melina clapped her hands together with excitement. "Oh, you have to come!" she insisted. "It's going to be so much fun! The whole gang is coming. Even Parker said he'd try to drop by!"

Logan didn't look quite as thrilled about that last part as Melina did. But he quickly gave Kris the address of his apartment before she could protest. "It's just a casual thing, no big deal. But it should be a blast. Promise you'll be there, okay?"

He looked at her searchingly and Kris felt a familiar blush rise on her cheeks as she gazed into his green eyes.

A party. That could be . . . interesting, she thought. It would be nice to have the chance to get to know Logan a little better away from the track. Maybe it would even help me figure out why I seem to get all crazy-happy every time I see him—if that means we have something in common, or if it's just a natural reaction to his being a total hottie. Either way, getting out will be good. It's about time I hang out with guys other than Junior and Matt.

"Well . . . maybe," Kris said, already trying to figure out what time she had to get up the following day and whether she had enough left over from last week's paycheck for bus fare into town. But looking up at Logan's hand-some face, she knew she'd have a hard time saying no. "Will you settle for an 'I'll try'?" she asked instead.

Logan pretended to pout. "Only if that's the best you can do," he said. Pointing to a man around Pablo's age who was hurrying down the aisle toward them, he added, "Even old

Jackson there promised to come. And he never goes anywhere. Head groom and all—thinks he's too good for us most of the time."

The man skidded to a stop in front of them. There was an anxious expression on his tanned, deeply lined face and he didn't appear to have heard Logan's joking comment. "Guys, did one of you take the Bute out of the medicine chest?"

"Not me," Logan said.

Melina looked up from her work long enough to shake her head. "Is it missing, or something?" she asked.

Jackson sighed and rubbed his partially bald, sunburned head. "Yeah. Last bottle—I placed an order for more yesterday, but it's not here yet. Didn't think I had to worry, since this one was almost full."

Kris immediately knew why the head groom looked so worried. Bute was another name for phenylbutazone, a common anti-inflammatory drug. Every medication cabinet at the track kept a bottle on hand for minor aches and pains or slight soreness, and many horses raced on it as a matter of course.

"Bummer," Logan said. "Can't you borrow some from another barn until the new shipment comes?"

"Of course I can," Jackson said with a frown. "But ours shouldn't be missing. Parker is pretty steamed about it."

Just then, Logan rested his arm on a stall door, and Kris's gaze fell on the face of his Rolex. It was getting late. "I'd better go," she said as Jackson stomped off down the aisle. "I need to meet Pablo soon. Hope you find the Bute!"

"But you just got here!" Melina cried.

"Don't worry," Logan said. "We'll see her at the party tonight. Right, Kris?" He stepped forward and touched Kris lightly on the arm.

Kris smiled, her skin tingling a little even after he pulled his hand away. "Like I said: I'll try." Spotting Beau stretching his big chestnut head out over his stall guard nearby, she stepped over to give the friendly horse a quick pat before she left.

"Oh, that reminds me," Melina said, pointing toward Beau with her pitchfork. "Beau's running the day after tomorrow. You should try to come watch."

"Definitely!" Kris said. "I'd love to see him run."

"So Beau gets a 'definitely' and the best you'll give me is an 'I'll try'?" Logan said. "Guess that tells me where I stand."

Kris grinned. "Guess so," she said, giving Beau one last pat and heading off down the aisle. "See you guys tonight—maybe."

Chapter Seven

That night, as Kris stepped into a crowded apartment, she couldn't help but wonder if she had the right address. There was definitely a party going on. Music was blasting so loudly the windows were rattling, and the place was packed with people chatting, drinking, and dancing. And if there was any doubt, she'd seen Logan's name on the mail slot downstairs. Somehow, though, the apartment itself wasn't quite what she'd been expecting.

So much for the whole being-disowned-by-parents thing, she thought, looking around at the spacious, high-ceilinged main room, with its expensive stereo system, big-screen TV, leather sofas, and classy paintings on the walls. Logan seems to be doing pretty well on a groom's salary.

Kris was so busy gawking at the place that she didn't notice a college-age guy carrying three overflowing plastic cups and bumped into him. He was wearing a T-shirt with Greek letters on it, along with a pair of expensive designer jeans and a flashy college ring.

"Hey, what the—" the guy began. Turning and getting a look at Kris, his angry expression faded into a leer. "Sorry, gorgeous," he said, his eyes traveling slowly up and down her body.

"It's okay," Kris mumbled, tugging at the hem of her skirt, which suddenly felt far too short. She had the unsettling feeling that she'd just stumbled into an alternate dimension— similar to her world, but not quite the same. It was the same reaction she had whenever she had to attend some snooty affair at the Davis ranch or any other gathering involving large numbers of wealthy people. It felt like she had a bull's-eye on her forehead that flashed "fair game" over and over again.

Looking around the place for a familiar

face, she spotted Logan standing in front of the window at the far end of the room. He was smiling and chatting with a pair of pretty girls wearing stylish, sexy outfits that probably cost more than what Kris made in a year.

Slowly, Kris started to back out of the apartment, hoping to escape before Logan saw her. Suddenly, going home and reading a magazine in her trailer seemed like the perfect evening. But just then she spotted Mac Mackenzie, Shorty, and a few other people from the racetrack, and she felt herself relax a little. Good, she thought. So there are some track people here, after all. I'm not completely alone.

As she hurried over to join them, Mac saw her and gave her a friendly wave. "Look, guys," he cried to his companions over the pulsing music. "It's the Raintree spy!"

"Uh-oh," a pixie-faced female groom named Joey joked. "Guess it's time to stop discussing all our training secrets."

"Very funny, guys," Kris said with a smile, her awkward feelings almost completely gone.

"Melina was wondering if you'd show," Mac

said. "She was just looking for you. I don't know where she—"

"Kris! You're here!" With a squeal, Melina appeared, racing up to give Kris a welcoming hug.

"Wow," Kris said as she stepped back and got a good look at Melina. She realized it was the first time she'd seen her new friend in anything except grungy old barn clothes. "You look amazing!"

"Likewise, toots," she said with a grin.

Melina really did look nice. Her unruly curls had been tamed, and her expressive hazel eyes looked bigger than usual thanks to carefully applied makeup. To complete the makeover, she'd traded in her jeans and T-shirt for a slinky blue dress that showed off her slim figure.

For the next few minutes, Melina kept everyone laughing by making fun of all the snotty guys and girls Logan had invited to the party. The whole time, though, Melina's eyes were constantly darting all over the apartment. She seemed to be looking for someone, and Kris had a pretty good idea who that *someone* might be.

"So is Parker here yet?" she asked casually,

after seeing Melina turn and stare at the door for about the tenth time.

"No. I really hope he shows—it took some convincing to get Logan to invite him." Melina frowned. "He said he'd try to make it."

Kris felt a flash of pity for her friend. It couldn't be easy for her, having a crush on the guy who was technically her boss. That was bound to complicate things. And even if Kris wasn't sure she saw Parker's appeal, she certainly knew how it felt to be stuck in a tricky romantic situation. For a second, she was tempted to share more of her own feelings about Matt, Junior, *and* Logan, but she held back. After all, Logan and Melina were friends—she didn't want to put either of them in an awkward situation, and she definitely did not need to complicate things any more by divulging too much information.

"Give him time," she said instead, hoping to raise Melina's spirits. "Maybe he's running fashionably late. That's the cool thing about a truly great party, right? You just never know who's going to show up—or when."

As the words left her mouth, she followed

Melina's gaze back to the door and froze in disbelief. Okay, I haven't had a thing to drink, so I shouldn't be seeing things, she thought. But I could swear that Dani and Amber just walked in!

"Hey," Melina said. "Aren't those the two snotty girls you know? What are *they* doing here?"

"I don't know." Kris wished she'd left to spend the evening with a magazine when she'd had the chance. But now it was too late; Dani and Amber had spotted her. They pushed their way through the crowd.

"Well, well," Dani said, stopping in front of Kris. "Look what we have here."

Amber swept back her hair with one hand, which set her bracelets jingling. Both she and Dani were wearing slinky dresses, high heels, and plenty of makeup, looking more ready for a big night out at a trendy club than hanging out at an apartment party. "Where's your boyfriend Logan?" she asked Kris with a smirk.

"Please!" Dani rolled her eyes. "Don't be cruel, Amber. You know nothing's ever going to come of Kris's pathetic crush on that boy.

100

It's not as if he has anything in common with a girl like her."

"What's that supposed to mean?" Kris demanded. She was getting tired of Dani's little digs implying that Kris wasn't good enough—first for Matt, then Junior, and now Logan. The girl was a one-woman hatefest.

Melina put a hand on her arm. "Chill," she said quietly. "They're not worth it."

Dani shot Melina a disdainful look and seemed ready to say something. But at that moment Amber let out a little gasp that verged on a squeal. "There's Logan," she said, grabbing Dani's arm. "And check out the hottie he's talking to! Come on, let's go say hi."

Without another word to Kris and Melina, they turned and skittered on their high heels over toward Logan. Kris smiled when she saw who Logan was talking to. It was the Greek-letters-shirt guy Kris had bumped into earlier. *It figures Amber would think a meathead like that is good-looking,* she thought. *But, hey, if she wants that, she can have it.*

And apparently *both* wanted that. Soon, Dani and Amber were smiling and tossing their hair at the two guys. Watching Amber throw back her head and let out a shriek of laughter that was audible even over the loud music, Kris gritted her teeth. And every time Dani flashed Logan her coy little smile or touched him on the arm, Kris was tempted to stomp across the room and fling her drink in the other girl's face, like someone from a TV soap opera.

"It's not that I'm not glad they're leaving us alone," she said to Melina after witnessing the fiftieth hair toss. "But I do feel kind of bad for Logan."

"Logan's a big boy. He can handle a couple of bimbos like them," Melina said distractedly, once again glancing toward the door. "So, what do you think could be keeping Parker? Maybe he forgot the party was tonight, or . . ."

For the next half an hour or so, Kris took sips from a cup of punch and listened to Melina complain about Parker's absence. Her only real entertainment, if she could call it that, was watching Dani and Amber out of the corner of her eye as they flirted their heads off with Logan and his friends.

It's not like I expected anything better from those two, she thought, wincing as Dani reached up to run her fingers through Logan's blond hair. But I did expect more from Logan, and he doesn't exactly look like he's hating all the attention.

She closed her eyes, wondering (not for the first time) if she'd been a fool to come. Sure, Logan had been nice to her at the track, flirted with her, acted like he was dying for her to come to this party.

But what did I think was going to happen tonight? she asked herself. Did I think he'd rush over as soon as I came in, ignore all his other guests because he was so glad to see me? Maybe declare his undying love and sweep me off my feet to live in luxury on his trust fund? Yeah. Nice fantasy, Furillo.

Just then Mac spilled his drink on himself and Kris made sure she laughed along with the others. But somehow, the party had lost its appeal.

As the hour got later, the music got louder, and the racetrack people started to say good night and leave in ones and twos. By that point, Kris had started thinking about saying good night herself. Logan still hadn't even noticed she was there, and maybe that was just as well.

"Want to get out of here?" she asked Melina after Mac said good-bye and left. "This party is going downhill, fast."

Melina answered, but her words were drowned out in a burst of extra-loud music. Kris glanced over and saw that Dani and Amber were standing in front of the stereo with a couple new meathead guys. One of them was hugging Amber, running his hands up and down her back, while the other was cranking up the music and laughing as Dani did a sexy little wriggle to the beat. Logan had disappeared.

"What did you say?" she asked Melina. "Ready to go?"

"I think I'll hang out for a while," Melina said, raising her voice over the stereo. "You know—just for a little bit longer."

Kris knew Melina was probably still hoping Parker would turn up. But she didn't feel like waiting around for him any longer herself.

"Okay, then," she told Melina, suddenly

feeling very tired. This evening hadn't turned out the way she'd expected, and she was ready to fall into bed and forget all about it. "I'm going to take off."

With a quick good-bye to her friend, she headed for the door. Several rowdy frat-boy types were doing some sort of weird interpretive dance in the middle of the floor, which mostly seemed to involve jumping up and down, flinging their arms around, and yelling at the top of their lungs. Since there wasn't really any way around them, Kris ducked her head and barged through, hoping a flailing arm would push her right through the crowd and out the door.

When she emerged on the far side of the mass of dancing guys, she found Logan there waiting for her. "There you are!" he exclaimed. "I have been looking for you *all* night."

"Not very hard," Kris countered, pushing back a strand of her dark hair. "I've been here for a couple of hours."

Logan smiled and took her arm. "My bad," he said. "Can I make it up to you by getting you a drink? Or maybe you'd rather dance?"

Kris hesitated. His expression was beseeching, and he looked cuter than ever in the dim party light. "I don't know. . . ." she began.

"Come on, beautiful." He moved a little closer. "You can't leave without one dance, can you? Don't make me get down on my knees and beg—you know I'll do it! I have no shame."

Kris couldn't help laughing as he started to get down on one knee. "Get up," she exclaimed. "I guess I could stick around for one dance. If it means so much to you."

"I knew you'd come around," Logan said with a grin. "Come on, I love this song. . . ."

Wrapping his arms around Kris's waist, he moved farther into the room and began humming along with the sound system. Kris lifted her arms to his shoulders as the two of them began to sway to the music. Despite the attention, she felt an uneasy shiver run up her spine

He knew I'd come around, she thought. Is that because a guy like Logan is used to getting whatever he wants? I mean, he talked me into coming to this party, and when I'm about to leave he convinces me to stay. . . .

She shook her head, smiling at her own

paranoia. First, she was upset that he was ignoring her, and now she was upset that he wasn't. Was it any wonder all her relationships seemed so complicated?

"What's so funny?" Logan whispered into her ear.

Kris glanced up at him, realizing he'd seen her smile. "Nothing," she said, turning her head and resting her cheek against the warm fabric of his shirt. "I was just thinking—I'm glad I came tonight."

"You and me both." Logan ran his hands up her back, pulling her even closer. "I don't know what it is, Kris, but I . . . I just like you. It's like we have a connection, you know? Does that sound like a totally cheesy thing to say?"

"No," Kris said softly. "It doesn't sound cheesy at all."

She looked up at him again. Their eyes locked, and the music seemed to fade away. The only beat Kris could hear now was the rhythm of her heart, which suddenly seemed to be racing along at double its usual rate.

Holding her breath, she tilted her head back. Logan's face moved closer . . . and a second later his lips brushed hers. Melting into the kiss, she was aware of nothing other than the feel of his lips, the faint scent of his cologne, and the press of his hands through her dress. He pulled her tighter against him and as she felt the kiss deepen, her hand reached up to touch his hair and . . .

Suddenly, Amber's familiar shriek cut through the breathless moment. "Logan! There you are!"

Kris's eyes flew open and she pulled back with a gasp. Logan blinked down at her, his face mirroring her own slightly confused expression. Pushing loose of his embrace, Kris glanced over and saw Dani and Amber dancing toward them, pink-cheeked and giggling. Dani shot Kris a disdainful glance, then pushed past her and draped her arms over Logan's shoulders.

"You promised me a dance, Logan," she said with a pout. "So how about it? Ready to boogie, big boy?"

"Um . . ." Logan looked uncertain. "Look, Dani. I was sort of in the middle of something just now."

Dani rolled her eyes. "Yeah, I could see that," she said. "But I'm here now. You don't have to slum it anymore. After all, you already know what kind of kisser *I* am, Logey-ogan. . . ."

What was that supposed to mean? Kris wondered, her face flaming. Has Logan been kissing every girl at this party? So much for a connection! Clearly he's been *connecting* all night!

"I've got to go," she blurted out, before turning and rushing toward the door, giving Logan no chance to respond.

"We're not going to hang around the racetrack all day, are we, Matt?" Amber whined, picking at a chip in her French manicure.

Kris scowled. Once again, she was squished into the backseat of Junior's car with Amber and Dani, while Junior and Matt sat up front. If I had anything to say about it, you wouldn't have to hang around the track at all, she thought.

It was the day of Beau's race, and Kris had

asked Matt to go with her. For one thing, she needed a ride. But she also figured having him along would give her an excuse to avoid dealing with Logan. After Dani's comment and her own abrupt exit from the party the other night, she wasn't sure she was ready to face him yet. But she was too excited about seeing big, sweet Beau do his thing to stay away from the track completely.

Unfortunately, even if she could avoid Logan until she got her thoughts in order, she still had to deal with Dani and Amber. She and Matt had started out in his truck, but then stopped along the way to get in Junior's Porsche—along with Dani and Amber. Somehow, the two girls had gotten wind of the trip and begged to come. And once he'd heard, Junior had invited himself along as well—the more the merrier, he'd said with a mischievous wink at Kris.

She had hoped to lose them once they got to the track, but to her dismay the whole group trailed after her to Beau's stall.

When they arrived, they found Beau standing in the aisle while Melina and Logan helped his primary groom, José, brush him down and get him ready to head over to the paddock. Parker was there as well, standing beside a sharply dressed man in his forties who was talking on a cell phone. Kris nodded hello, and then waved at Melina, who looked just as busy as all the others. Logan glanced over at her, too, and gave her a wink, but Kris quickly dropped her eyes. Now that she was standing right here in front of him again, the party—and its awkward ending—came rushing back to her. Part of her was glad Logan at least winked at her—maybe he didn't think she was a total wierdo—but she was also glad that he was too busy to talk to her. By the time he had a free moment, maybe she'd have figured out what to say to him about their kiss . . . and *his* kiss with Dani.

"Check it out," Matt whispered into Kris's ear, nodding toward the other man. "That's Jeff Trenton."

Kris shot the older man a curious glance, but her gaze quickly returned to Beau. The big colt was standing quietly, one hind foot cocked and his head hanging and relaxed, while the humans dashed here and there all around him. He seemed completely unfazed by all the activity. Kris was impressed. *Wildfire doesn't stand that calmly right after a hard workout,* she thought, *let alone right before heading out to the track!*

"Wow, he really is a quiet one, huh?" Junior commented, obviously thinking along the same lines. "He doesn't even seem to realize it's race day."

"Oh, he knows," Melina said breathlessly. "He just doesn't let it get to him."

José nodded. "He lets us do all the worrying for him."

Nearby, Dani sidled closer to Logan, who was brushing out Beau's tail. "What a good-looking horse."

Logan glanced at her, looking a bit harried. This was not really the time or the place for flirting and he knew it—even if Dani chose to ignore it. "Yeah, he's great," he said shortly.

Meanwhile, Amber walked right up to Parker. "Hi, again," she greeted him with a coy smile. "Remember me?"

If Kris had had any doubts about why the pair had wanted to come to the track, they were gone now. "Maybe we should get out of the way," she said pointedly, making sure her voice was loud enough for Dani and Amber to hear. "These guys have a lot to do."

Amber glanced at her and took a tiny half-step back from Parker. Dani, on the other hand, completely ignored her.

Typical Dani behavior, Kris thought. Like she of all people doesn't have *any* idea how important the prerace atmosphere is. But, if the two girls were going to stand around flirting and getting in the way, it didn't mean she had to watch. There were still a few minutes before Beau had to head over to the paddock.

That should give me just enough time for a quick visit with Wildfire, she told herself. And that sounds a whole lot more pleasant than sticking around here in Awkwardville.

She told the others where she was going, and Matt offered to walk her over. "I told Mom I'd check in on the Raintree horses while I was here," he explained.

Leaving the group behind, they walked through the backside to the barn where Raintree had several stalls. Wildfire had his head hanging out into the aisle taking in the sights, but he turned and let out a snort when Kris whistled to him.

She smiled. "That's my boy," she murmured, hurrying to let herself into the stall while Matt wandered off down the row to check on the other horses. "Now for a little quality time."

However, Wildfire's version of quality time didn't seem to agree with her own. From the moment she entered the stall, the lanky bay horse barely stood still for a second. He grabbed a bite from his haynet, then barged forward to stare out at the horse in the aisle. Then, he ducked back into his stall, ignoring Kris as she reached up to scratch his withers.

"Hey!" she said sharply, feeling a flash of irritation. "Stand still, would you?"

But Wildfire continued to ignore her and shoved his nose into his full water bucket, sending its contents flying everywhere. Kris jumped back just in time to avoid getting soaked, but she wasn't quick enough to avoid the spray of water when Wildfire suddenly turned and blew out a loud snort in her direction.

"Ew! Thanks a lot," she complained, brushing at her shirt and jeans. "Wildfire, would you just relax?"

In response, he charged to the front of his stall again, ears pricked forward. Outside, a hot-walker was leading a petite rose-gray filly past the stall. Wildfire let out an earsplitting whinny and when the other horse responded, he tossed his head and leaped backward, almost crashing into Kris.

"Okay, okay," Kris muttered, pushing past the jumpy horse to the front of the stall. "I can take a hint. Maybe you're not in the mood for—hey!"

She cut herself off as Wildfire grabbed another mouthful of hay and then lurched to the side, one of his metal-shod hooves almost landing on the toe of her sneaker. She yanked her foot out of the way just in time.

"Quit it!" she exclaimed. "Why can't you just stand still like Beau once in a while?"

"Everything okay in here?"

Matt was standing outside the stall door, a worried look on his face. He pushed Wildfire's head aside as the horse nosed at him.

"It's nothing," Kris muttered, embarrassed by the outburst Matt had most likely heard.

Matt looked at her closely, and Kris felt a familiar flush rise on her cheeks. "There aren't many racehorses as quiet as Beau," he said calmly. "Besides, Wildfire's still pretty new to this whole living-at-the-track thing. He'll settle as he gets used to all the activity."

"Yeah, you're probably right." Kris forced a smile on her face. What had she been thinking? How could she compare Wildfire to Beau like that? It wasn't fair. Letting herself out of the stall, she tried to shrug the guilt off by changing the subject. "We should get back to Trenton's and make sure Dani and Amber aren't getting in the way too much."

She gave Wildfire one last pat, dodging as he swung his head at her. Then with a sigh, she and Matt hurried back to the Trenton Stables area.

They arrived to find greater pandemonium than before they left. Parker and the grooms were racing around shouting, while Junior, Amber, and Dani looked on. Jeff Trenton was standing in the middle of the aisle staring at Beau, who looked as relaxed as ever.

"Everything under control?" Matt asked Junior as Parker and Logan disappeared in one direction and Melina in the other, leaving only José and Trenton standing with the horse.

"Not really," Junior replied. "They can't find Beau's blinkers. I guess he has custom-made extra-large ones for his big old head, and they're not in the tack stall where they should be."

Melina rushed back from wherever she'd gone just in time to overhear Junior's explanation. "We have tons of other blinkers," she said breathlessly, her hazel eyes anxious, "but they won't fit Beau. He'd probably go okay without, but it's too late to register an equipment change. We need to find them in the next ten minutes or he'll have to scratch!"

Jeff Trenton heard her. "We're not going to scratch," he said with a slight frown. "Parker said they were here an hour ago. That means they still have to be here. Now go find them!"

"Yikes," Kris said quietly to Matt and Junior as Melina raced off in the direction of the tack stall. "These guys must be having a bad week.

First that filly gets loose, then the Bute goes missing. . . ."

Kris had been trying to keep her voice quiet, but Trenton heard her. "Yes," he said thoughtfully, his ice blue eyes boring straight into hers. "I heard all about those problems. And I'm starting to think someone around here might be a jinx."

Chapter Eight

Kris's face flamed. She wasn't sure whether the poker-faced trainer was serious, or if he was even referring to her at all. Luckily, she didn't end up having to find out. Just then, Trenton's cell phone rang, and he quickly put it to his ear and moved away.

"Okay, that was a little awkward," Junior said when the trainer was out of earshot. "Was he talking about you, Kris?"

Kris shrugged. She knew superstitions were a serious thing for a lot of people at the track. The last thing she wanted was for her new friends at Trenton Stables to consider her a jinx.

What if Trenton really does think I had

something to do with all those problems? she wondered. What if he thinks that I'm intentionally hurting his barn? After all, I do seem to be around a lot when stuff happens. If word got out that I was a jinx or even just the hint of a rumor started, it could mean the end of hanging out at the track.

She chewed her lower lip, immediately wondering if Trenton had heard about her past somehow. It wouldn't be the first time someone had jumped to conclusions about her after hearing she had a police record. And sadly, it wouldn't be the first time someone pointed a finger.

The thought made her angry. Why did people have to be so judgmental? Sometimes it seemed as if she'd never be able to escape from the mistakes she'd made in her past, no matter how hard she worked at it.

Just then Logan came racing back into the aisle. "I've turned the tack room upside down," he gasped out, red-faced and panting. "Those blinkers aren't there! Just the regular-sized ones." He held up several sets of blinkers embroidered in Trenton Stables' colors.

"Just great. What are we going to do now?" Melina exclaimed, having just gotten back from her search.

José looked up from brushing a speck of dirt off Beau's left leg. "We don't have much time," he said, reaching out to take one of the fabric blinker hoods from Logan. "Maybe we can adjust these somehow, or—"

"I found them!" Parker's voice rang through the shedrow, interrupting all other conversation. A second later, he appeared at the end of the aisle, holding up a set of extra-large blinkers.

Everyone started talking at once. Kris let out a breath of relief and glanced at Junior and Matt. "Whew, that was close."

"I wonder where they were," Matt said.

He didn't have to wait long for an answer. "What I want to know," Parker went on, even as José grabbed the blinkers and started putting them on Beau, "is why I found Beau's blinkers stuffed between two bales in the hay stall?"

"Huh?" Logan blinked. "How'd they end up there?"

Parker glared at him. "That's my point, bright guy," he snapped. "I seriously doubt they floated there by themselves. Someone didn't want us to find them."

"Maybe." Melina sounded dubious. "But it could've just been someone's dog dragging them off, or . . ."

"He's ready," José interrupted as he finished buckling Beau's bridle. "We have to go. Now."

Some of Kris's excitement about the race began to return as she and the others followed Beau and his entourage down the long dirt path to the paddock, where the horses were saddled before each race.

As José led the big chestnut into the paddock, accompanied by Trenton and Parker, the rest of them stopped outside, finding a place along the rail to watch. Kris ended up standing between Matt and Melina, while farther down the rail she could hear Dani and Amber giggling and flirting with Logan.

"He looks good, doesn't he?" Melina asked, her eyes glued to Beau.

Kris nodded. "He looks great."

Junior had been standing a short distance

away, studying the race program he'd just pulled out of his back pocket. "Hey," he said, coming over to the others. "You guys feel pretty good about the big guy, right?"

Melina and Logan both nodded. "He'll win easy," Logan said confidently.

"Cool." Junior grinned. "In that case, I've got a few bucks I'm going to put on him before betting closes."

"I'll come with you," Matt said. "We'll meet you guys out front for the race, okay?"

"We'll come with you, too," Amber said, grabbing Dani. "I need a Diet Coke, stat."

Dani looked annoyed to be pulled away from Logan, but she went along as the others hurried off toward the grandstand building. Kris wasn't sorry to see them go, though she quickly realized that she was now alone with Melina *and* Logan. She cast Logan a weary glance, still not feeling ready to talk about the party.

But to her relief, Logan didn't seem to be thinking about that. "Weird about the blinkers, huh?" he commented, leaning on the rail right next to Kris. "I wonder what happened."

"I don't know," Melina said. "But Parker didn't need that—especially with Mr. Trenton here today."

Logan smirked. "No kidding," he said. "But he probably also didn't need Kris's superintellectual blond friend hanging off his arm." He glanced over and winked playfully at Kris. "Although, he didn't look all that upset about that."

"Friend?" Kris snorted as Melina frowned and punched Logan in the arm. "Amber? Not hardly."

"Aw, come on!" Logan feigned surprise. "But you two clearly have *so* much in common! And Amber and Dani both have such sweet things to say about you."

"Yeah, I bet," Kris muttered. But she found herself smiling. She was relieved that Logan didn't seem to take Dani and Amber seriously. Somehow, she'd assumed otherwise after seeing them together at the party. It didn't help matters that the three of them all came from similar backgrounds—backgrounds very different from her own. But now, knowing that Logan could take them for what they were, Kris felt a lot better about everything. She hadn't *completely* misjudged him.

I just wish I knew what he thought about me, she thought. Does he *like me*, like me? Or, is he feeling just the whole friend vibe? He really just needs to let me know what he's thinking—before I go totally insane.

Luckily, Kris had the race to distract her. A few minutes later, the horses were all tacked up and the paddock steward called for riders up. "We'd better get out front so we don't miss the post parade," Melina said. "I want to check out Beau's competition."

"Beau has no competition," Logan said confidently. "He's going to smoke 'em."

They hurried over to the apron area in front of the grandstand. Matt and the others had already found a spot along the rail, and Kris, Logan, and Melina joined them just as the outrider's horse started across the expanse of the homestretch with the nine horses entered in the race straggling along in a more-or-less straight row behind him. Several of the racers were jigging and prancing. To Kris's surprise,

Beau was among them. His legs flew in all directions as he trotted along with his head straight up in the air. When a bird flew past over the track he spooked sideways, crashing into the stout buckskin lead pony walking along beside him.

"Uh-oh!" Kris said. "What's wrong with him?"

"Yeah, really." Junior looked worried as he glanced from the betting ticket in his hand to the big chestnut horse, who had just flung his head to the ground, almost ripping the reins out of his jockey's hands. "He's totally freaking out!"

"What?" Melina looked confused for a second. Then her face cleared. "Oh, that's right! You guys haven't actually seen him during the post parade yet."

"Beau is a saint ninety-nine percent of the time," Logan explained. "Grooming, tacking, walking him out before the race—he's cool as a cucumber. But the post parade . . . Well, he can be a bit of a handful."

"He'll settle once he's at the gate," Melina said. "You'll see."

Out on the track, Beau had just reared up and then skittered sideways, again banging against his patient lead pony.

Matt leaned toward Kris. "See?" he said quietly. "Maybe you don't want Wildfire to act just like him, after all."

Kris knew he was trying to make her feel better about her comment in Wildfire's stall earlier. But it wasn't really working. She had doubted Wildfire—and it felt terrible no matter what Matt said.

She pushed the thought aside as the horses finished the post parade and warm-up and headed back around to the starting gate. True to Melina's word, Beau seemed to settle down as soon as the parade was over. As he neared the gate, he stopped jigging and allowed an assistant starter to take his bridle and lead him into the number one slot. He loaded easily and stood quietly while all the other horses entered their stalls.

"Here goes nothing," Melina said, quickly touching her nose and then her chin several times. When Dani gave her a perplexed look, she said, "For luck."

"Uh-huh." Dani rolled her eyes and turned away.

Just then the bell rang, the starting gate flew open, and the track announcer howled, "They're off!"

Beau broke alertly, surging ahead to share the lead with two other horses. The three of them quickly put several lengths between them and the rest of the pack, and things stayed that way all the way down the backstretch.

"He's looking good so far!" Kris cried, leaning against the rail in front of her.

"Go, Beau, go, Beau, go!" Melina chanted.

Junior clutched his betting ticket. "Get up there!" he added. "Daddy needs a new set of speakers for his Porsche!"

On the turn, two horses broke free of the pack to challenge Beau and the others. "That's Cal City Cal coming on the outside," the track announcer cried. "Shoptilyoudrop is right with him. They've caught the leaders, just as Mortgage Lender is dropping back. . . ."

Kris squinted against the California sun as she tried to see what was happening. When that didn't work, she shifted her gaze to the big screen in the middle of the infield just in time to see Beau put his head in front of the other horses.

"There he goes!" Logan cried, pumping his fist. "Halfway around the turn, just like clockwork!"

Beau crept forward on the rail as he rounded the turn, pulling away from the others, stride by stride. He hit the long, straight expanse of the homestretch with a two-length advantage. Kris saw his ears prick forward. He swapped smoothly from his left lead to his right, the jockey tapped him once with the whip—and with that, Beau exploded forward.

"Whoa!" Matt cried as a howl of excitement went up from the grandstand. "Look at him go!"

It was as if Beau had just decided to start running. His stride lengthened, eating up the remaining furlongs. Soon, the closest of the field was four lengths behind him, then five.

". . . and it's Loyal Beau by seven!" the track announcer cried as Beau swept smoothly under the finish line all alone.

Realizing she'd been holding her breath for the last furlong, Kris let it out in a gasp. "He was amazing!" she exclaimed to Melina.

"Yeah!" Amber said, looking impressed for once. "Wasn't that the horse we saw earlier? He was awesome!"

"He totally was!" Logan grinned and grabbed her in a hug. Amber giggled and hugged him back. That led to a flurry of hugging and hand-shaking, with everyone grinning and talking at once. Kris hugged Matt, then let out a gasp as Junior grabbed her in a tight squeeze.

"Oh, please," Dani said, rolling her eyes as Matt turned and grabbed her for a hug. "You'd think you guys had never seen a horse race before."

Kris ignored her, grinning and pushing Junior away as he moved his hands down her back, clearly trying to get a little bonus mileage out of his hug. "Enough!" she chided him. "The race was exciting, but not *that* exciting!"

"Can't blame a guy for trying." As Junior shrugged good-naturedly and turned away to hug Melina, Kris found herself facing Logan. He held out his arms.

"My turn?" he asked.

Kris blushed, suddenly all too aware of the proximity of the others—especially Junior and Matt—as Logan pulled her close. She shivered as she felt his warm breath on her neck, her mind once again filled with the memory of their kiss.

Maybe it wasn't exactly the perfect moment, but she suddenly felt the need to say something to him about what had happened between them. "Sorry about the other night," she murmured into his shirt. "I kind of acted like a fool. It was just that when Dani started blabbing about how you guys had kissed, I guess I thought, you know . . ."

He pulled away and glanced down at her. "Dani and I never kissed," he said, looking perplexed. "What do you—Oh!" His expression cleared. "I remember now. She didn't mean it like that. See, she'd just finished telling me some long, weird story about her first kiss back in middle school. . . ."

"Oh!" Kris exclaimed, feeling her cheeks go pink. "I totally thought—well, never mind. I'm even more sorry now."

Logan smiled at her. "Don't be."

He gave her arm one last squeeze, then turned to say something to Matt. Kris blinked, wondering if that was really all there was to it. Was he willing to forget about the kiss and awkward moment completely? And if so, did that mean it was just a one-time thing?

I guess this romance is going straight toward the platonic track, she thought. *Figures— unrequited crushes seem to be my thing.*

Wandering back toward the rail, her thoughts turned back to the race. She watched Beau come down to a jog far around the track and turn to return to the winner's circle. Once again he was back to his calm self. He trotted past the other racers breezing past him in the other direction without so much as a flick of the ear.

Melina ran over and grabbed Kris. "I'm so glad you came to see that," she said happily.

Kris smiled and hugged her back. "Me, too. Now come on—let's go get our picture taken!"

Chapter Nine

A couple of days later, Kris was mixing the morning grain in Raintree's feed room when she heard the sound of running feet outside. She glanced up just in time to see Todd skid around the corner into the room.

"Kris!" the little boy cried, sounding out of breath and anxious. "I was hoping you'd be in here!"

"What's wrong?" Kris asked.

Todd was an alert and barn-savvy kid. He wasn't the type to go racing around at top speed without reason.

Todd flopped down on a stack of feed bags, still gasping for breath. "I just heard Mom and Pablo talking," he said. "They were saying they need to do something about Gent."

Kris froze. She'd been so busy since the day of Beau's race that she'd barely had time to think about the fence problem. "How did they sound when they said it?" she asked.

"Serious," Todd replied. "They think he's going to ruin all the fences in his pasture by cribbing. What if they decide to send him away?"

"They can't do that," Kris said, automatically reaching over to stir the beet pulp soaking in a bucket in the sink while she tried to absorb Todd's news. She had never told Todd about Gent's situation and it was clear she should have. The youngest Ritter loved all the horses and the thought of one of them leaving really upset him. "They don't know for sure that he's the one doing the damage, do they?"

"I don't know." Todd bit his lip. "It sounds like they're pretty sure. But it's weird—I've been going down there almost every day to feed apples to the babies. You know, to help them be happy and forget that they're away from their mothers. Anyway, in all those times, I've never, ever seen Gent cribbing on the fence!"

"I haven't, either," Kris said, pretending to

know nothing of Todd's apple-feeding visits. "And I get the feeling Pablo hasn't, either. He's just assuming it's Gent because he cribs in his stall. Listen, Todd—maybe you can help convince Pablo and your mom to give Gent another chance. Are you going to feed apples to the babies again today?"

"Probably," Todd said. "I have a doctor's appointment in a little while. But I figured I'd go down there when I get back."

"Good." Kris smiled at him, then checked her watch. She still had a lot to do before she was supposed to meet Pablo at the ranch's training track to ride a couple of horses, so she'd have to leave the investigating to Todd. "While you're there, watch the whole herd carefully, okay? See if you can figure out which of them is really doing the cribbing or chewing or whatever. If we can convince Pablo and your mom that it's one of the weaners, they're liable to just let it slide. But if it *is* Gent . . ."

She let the sentence trail off. No! I can't think like that yet. We'll figure out the truth, she thought. And whatever consequences that brings, we'll just have to deal.

By the time Todd found her stacking hay later that afternoon, Kris had almost forgotten about Gent—again. She finished hoisting a heavy bale to the top of the pile, then jumped down and walked over to the boy.

"What's the word?" she asked, brushing her hands off on her jeans. "Did you solve the mystery?"

"Not really." Todd sighed loudly. "I took a bag of apples down today, and some carrots, too. I was there for, like, an hour watching. But none of the horses chewed on the fence at all."

Kris felt a flash of disappointment. She'd been hoping that Todd's surveillance would help clear things up. "Oh, well," she said. "Thanks for trying. At least you can tell Pablo and your mom that Gent's not out there cribbing nonstop."

"I guess." Todd didn't sound very heartened by that. But suddenly his face brightened. "Oh, I almost forgot—Grandpa said I could invite you to the track with us. He thought you might want to visit Wildfire."

"You mean, right now?" Kris glanced at her

watch. "I'd love to, but I still have another row to stack."

"That's okay," Todd said. "We can wait a few more minutes. We're just going over so Grandpa can drop off a check and I can test out my new stopwatch." He pulled a shiny silver disk out of his pocket and flipped it open, revealing a high-tech digital face. "See? I bought it with my allowance."

Kris smiled, amused as always by the little boy's seriousness about racing. While everyone at Raintree expected Matt to take over the business someday, he had confided in Kris that he wasn't sure he even wanted to stay in California. But Todd? He was a whole different story.

Jean doesn't have to worry about Todd not sticking around, Kris thought fondly. *This place is in his blood, just like it's in hers and Henry's. I can't imagine he will ever want to leave.*

"That sounds great," she told him, reaching out to ruffle his hair as she headed outside for another bale. "I promise, I'll have the rest of the hay stacked in record time. You can go ahead and test your new stopwatch on that!"

Kris, Henry, and Todd had barely set foot in the grandstand before they heard a raspy voice shouting out Henry's name. Turning, Kris saw a portly man around Henry's age coming toward them. He was walking with the help of a polished ebony cane and had a broad smile on his loose-jowled face.

"Henry Ritter, I can't believe that's you!" the man exclaimed when he reached them. "How long has it been, you bony old coot?"

"Charlie Coleman, you foulmouthed old rascal!" Henry responded, shaking the other man's hand vigorously. "You mean, you're still alive? I thought your bad temper would've killed you by now."

Kris's eyes widened, and she shot a surprised glance at Todd. Henry was usually soft-spoken and kind; she'd never heard that sort of talk from him before.

But the stranger, Charlie, just snorted with laughter at Henry's words and smacked his knee. "Only the good die young, don't you know?" he said. "Ah, Henry, it's been too long! How about if I buy you a drink at the bar?"

Henry hesitated, then shook his head. "Sorry, Charlie," he said. "I've already got plans with the kids here."

Kris could tell Henry was disappointed at having to say no. "That's okay," she spoke up. "If you want to go have a drink, I can keep an eye on Todd for a while."

"I can keep an eye on myself," Todd said. "I'm not some infant who needs a full-time babysitter, you know."

Henry smiled at him, then turned to Kris. "Are you sure you wouldn't mind?" he asked.

"The young lady just said so, Henry, you deaf old fool," Charlie said. "Now come on, before I change my mind about buying."

Henry's reply was lost in the crackle of the PA system announcing the results of the latest race. Giving Kris and Todd a wave, he walked off with his friend.

Kris waved back, then grabbed Todd's hand. "Come on, let's go to the backside," she said.

"Are we going to visit Wildfire first?" Todd asked.

"Of course!" Kris stated. "Where else would we go?"

Todd shrugged, looking a little surprised by her vehement answer. "I don't know," he said. "But remember, I need to test my stopwatch sometime."

"Right." Kris softened, realizing she was feeling a little defensive—perhaps because her first thought actually hadn't been of seeing Wildfire, but of heading over to say hi to Melina. "We'll do that in a little bit, okay? It sounds like a race just finished, so we have some time to kill, anyway."

They found Wildfire dozing in his stall, but he perked up when Kris let herself in, after firmly ordering Todd to stay right outside. Wildfire was normally gentle enough for a child to handle, but he was still a young, fit racehorse who didn't know his own strength. Besides, the way he'd jumped around the last time she'd visited hadn't exactly instilled confidence in her.

Fortunately, the big bay seemed to be in a much calmer mood today. He nuzzled at her hair as she gave him a hug and then set about brushing bits of straw out of his mane. When Todd pulled a piece of carrot out of his pocket, Wildfire lipped it carefully off his palm and then chewed it calmly.

A few minutes later, Wildfire's track groom arrived to take him for a walk. Kris wished she could offer to walk him herself, but she quickly decided it wouldn't be safe with Todd around. So instead, she figured it was time to go visit Melina. Giving Wildfire one last hug, she and Todd headed for the Trenton Stables shedrow.

"You'll love these guys," she told Todd. "They're supernice. And their big horse, Beau, is a total sweetheart."

"Kris!" Melina called as soon as the pair rounded the corner. "Hi, there. Who's your good-looking friend?"

Todd blushed, then grinned. "Hi," he said. "I'm Todd Ritter, future horse trainer. Who are you?"

Melina laughed. Brushing her hair out of her eyes, she leaned down to shake Todd's hand. "They call me Melina," she said. "I'll be your head groom someday. How's that sound?"

"Great!" Todd answered.

Kris smiled. "Okay, enough business talk," she joked. "I just brought Todd by to meet everyone, especially Beau."

"Step right this way," Melina said, putting a hand on Todd's shoulder. "I'll introduce you myself."

When they reached Beau's stall, they found José there wrapping the colt's legs. Kris introduced Todd, and then the boy gave Beau a pat as the horse stretched out his nose curiously. "Wow, his head is almost as big as I am," Todd said. He turned to José. "What's his registered name?"

"Loyal Beau," José replied. "He's by Beau Genius, out of a—"

"Storm Cat mare," Todd finished before José could. "I know. I read about his new track record in *Daily Racing Form* last month. He beat the old one by two-fifths of a second, right? And that was his third win in a row—if I recall correctly, his record is eight wins, one place, two shows out of thirteen races. Or was it twelve races?"

José straightened up, his impassive face

showing interest for the first time since Kris had met him. "It's twelve," he said. "Only finished out of the money once. Very impressive, kid. You know your stuff."

Just then Logan appeared, pushing a wheelbarrow stacked high with bags of sweet feed. He looked sweaty and dirty and totally gorgeous, and Kris couldn't help feeling a flutter in her stomach as she watched him unload one of the bags, setting it carefully against the wall out of reach of any of the nearby horses' hungry noses. She pushed aside the butterflies as he brushed off his hands and walked over to say hi. Kris introduced him to Todd.

"Remember this kid's name, son," José told Logan. "He'll be running this place someday."

Logan chuckled. "In that case, future boss, maybe I should show you around." He winked at Kris as he grabbed the handles of his wheelbarrow. "Come on, I'll give you the grand tour."

With Kris and Melina trailing along, Logan led Todd down to the end of the row and around the corner to the next aisle, where he delivered the rest of the feed to a fellow groom waiting at a storage stall. Then he showed

Todd around the rest of that aisle, introducing him to passing people and stopping to meet several of the other horses. Kris couldn't help smiling at the way Logan acted toward Todd, as if the two of them were old buddies, just like Henry and his friend Charlie.

Totally cute, she thought as Logan laughed at something Todd had just said and clapped him on the back. Just like everything else about Logan . . .

Ever since their quick chat after Beau's win the other day, Kris had decided to try to relax, stop worrying, and just enjoy her friendship—or whatever—with Logan. Even though it was hard to ignore the fact that Logan was a great, not to mention cute, guy, she was trying not to overthink what had happened or might happen between them. So far it seemed to be working—she found herself laughing and smiling almost nonstop as Logan continued to play tour guide for Todd and not focusing *too* much on her racing heart. It might not be easy, but she could do the friend thing if she had to. After all, hadn't she done it with Matt? And Junior, in a way?

They were watching the head groom, Jackson, deworm a squirmy filly when they heard an angry shout from the next aisle back. Melina glanced up worriedly. "That sounded like Parker," she said. "I'd better go see what's up."

Kris and Todd, along with the others, followed as she hurried back around the corner to the other aisle. When they arrived, they found Parker standing near Beau's stall, staring at something on the ground. His back was to them, and at first Kris wasn't sure what he was angry about.

Then he turned around and spotted them. Parker's face was drawn into an angry scowl as he pointed downward.

"Who did it?" he yelled. "Who spilled this feed all over the ground?"

Chapter Ten

Kris let out a gasp at Parker's words. Looking closer, she saw that one of the feed bags Logan had dropped off in the aisle earlier was now tipped over and ripped open. Sweet feed was scattered across the ground, mixing with dirt and straw and other debris. Several of the horses on the row, including Beau, were stretching their necks over their stall guards, doing their best to reach the spilled feed. Kris had been around horses long enough to know that if any of the Thoroughbreds had eaten too much of the feed, it could have been devastating. They could have colicked . . . or even worse, died.

At the sound of Parker's angry cries, people

had begun to run into the aisle. Mac was one of the last to arrive.

"Oh!" Mac said when he saw the cause of concern. His worried expression faded quickly. "You scared me, boss. I thought another horse was loose or something, not just a little feed accident."

"Listen, people," Parker exclaimed, his voice loud and his expression stormy. "There have been way too many 'accidents' around this barn lately, and I'm sick of it. This is a professional racing stable, not a circus." As he scowled around at all of them, his gaze fell on Todd, who was standing beside Kris. "Or a nursery school," he spat out, glaring at Todd and then at Kris. "We all need to shape up and get things running smoothly again, or Mr. Trenton will have to hear about it." He paused, this time glaring at each of his employees in turn. "Make sure this mess is cleaned up by the time I get back from the track office."

There was a moment of silence as Parker spun on his heel, stalked off, and disappeared around the corner. Then, Logan let out a low whistle.

"Talk about an overreaction!" he said. "It's not like a bag of feed has never gotten spilled before in the history of professional racing barns."

Melina shrugged, already bending down to sweep a bite of dirty feed out of reach of a long-necked filly stretching out of her stall. "I don't know," she said. "He has a point. We *have* been having a lot of stupid accidents this past week or two." As she straightened up, she glanced at Kris. "Come to think of it, you've been around for most of them, Kris."

Kris blinked. Is Melina serious? she wondered. It's bad enough that Parker and Mr. Trenton both seem to think I'm behind the trouble. Now Melina is starting to believe that, too? I just can't win. I am always going to be thought of as the ex-con.

Before Kris had the chance to defend herself, Shorty appeared at the end of the aisle leading a dark bay gelding. Seeing all of them standing there, he wandered over.

"What's goin' on?" he drawled. "Someone forgit to invite me to the party?"

While the others explained what had

happened, Kris stepped forward to help Melina, who was sweeping the spilled feed back into the bag. Todd dropped to his knees to help as well. While she was tempted to say something to Melina about her comment, Kris held her tongue, not wanting to get into it in front of Todd.

"That Parker guy seemed really mad," Todd commented as he scooped up a mixture of feed and dirt and dumped it into the bag.

Melina glanced over at him. "Yeah, he did," she said. "It's only because this whole bag of feed is ruined now, plus if the horses had gotten into it they could've gotten really sick."

Todd nodded wisely. "Colic," he said. "Or founder."

"Right." Melina smiled slightly. "You really are a smart kid, you know that?" Then her smile faded, and she sighed. "Maybe *you* can figure out what's jinxing us lately."

As she spoke, Melina shot Kris a glance. That was it! Kris had had enough—Melina was supposed to be her friend. "Why don't you just come out and say it?" she challenged Melina, trying to keep her voice low so the other Trenton employees wouldn't overhear. "It's obvious Parker thinks I'm the jinx—or maybe the one who's pulling all this bad stuff. Is that what you think, too? I always seem to be around at the wrong time, right? You said it yourself."

Melina's hazel eyes widened. "What?" she cried. "Kris, no! That wasn't what I meant at all!"

Kris rocked back on her heels, glaring at Melina. "Really?" she snapped. "Then what *did* you mean? Come on, I was here when that horse got loose, right? And when the Bute went missing, and the blinkers, and now this. . . ." She waved a hand at the spilled feed. "Between that and my police record, is it any surprise everyone is looking my way? Is it any surprise Parker practically came right out and accused me of dumping his stupid grain all over the ground?"

As she went on, her voice had risen, and a couple of people were now shooting curious glances in their direction. Melina grabbed Kris's arm, pulling her closer and speaking quietly enough so that only she and Todd could hear.

"Listen, Kris," she said, her tone and eyes serious. "I don't care what everyone thinks or doesn't think. *I* know you didn't have anything to do with these problems."

Kris felt some of her anger start to melt away.

"I was trying to make a joke," Melina continued, looking sheepish and worried. "A lame joke, I admit. But Parker was so mad and everyone was so tense—I thought I might be able to lighten the mood, I guess."

"I know you'd never do something like this, Kris," Todd added. "You're too honest. If you'd done it, you would've admitted it right away." He glanced down at the feed. "Besides, there's no way you could've spilled this stuff. You were with me and Melina and Logan the whole time."

"That's true." Hearing Todd's words, Kris felt a little better. "So I guess there's no way Parker can pin this terrible crime on one of us, huh? He'll have to call in the FBI to find himself another suspect to prosecute."

Melina laughed with relief. "That's more like it," she said. "Anyway, Parker will cool off soon and realize that sometimes things just happen. He has a quick temper, but he's not stupid. Come to think of it, he's got to realize you couldn't have done most of the stuff he was ranting about. You weren't here when Rosie got out of her stall—you were with me, remember?"

"You're right. I'm sorry for freaking out like that," Kris said. "I guess I'm just a little sensitive about stuff like this. You know—because of my past. That's why I thought everyone was blaming me."

"Does everyone know about that?" Todd asked, shooting Melina a curious look.

"Only me," Melina told him with a sly smile. "Kris told me about Camp LaGrange and all that. I meant to post the whole story on the barn bulletin board, but I forgot. So those guys don't know anything about it." She gestured toward the other employees, most of whom were still discussing what had just happened.

Todd's eyes widened in surprise. "You were going to put that on the *bulletin board*?"

Kris laughed. "She's just teasing, Todd,"

she said, giving him a pat on the knee.

But Kris couldn't help but wonder if Parker had found out about her past somehow. Word got around fast at the track. If Henry let something slip to one of his friends, or if Matt or Junior did, it could easily have gotten back to someone like Parker. And what about big-mouthed Dani and Amber? They could have said something to Parker just to make Kris look bad.

Looking down at the spilled sweet feed, Kris frowned. It hurt knowing that there probably wasn't anything she could do to change some people's minds about her. If they wanted to believe she was some kind of criminal because of what had happened in the past, they would just keep on believing it no matter what.

I guess it's just something I'm always going to have to deal with, she thought with a sigh, *thanks to those few bad choices I made once upon a time. . . .*

Chapter Eleven

A few days later, Kris was waiting at the Raintree gate when Junior's Porsche skidded up in a spray of gravel. He was heading to the track to watch some of his father's horses run and had asked Kris to come along. Giving her a cheerful wave, he threw the car into neutral while from the passenger seats, Dani and Amber scowled at her in surprise.

"I thought we were here to pick up Matt." Dani glared at her brother accusingly over the top of her designer sunglasses as Kris stepped toward the car. "Not *her.*"

"Oh, did I forget to tell you? Turns out, Matt's busy today," Junior replied. "But lucky for us, Kris agreed to grace us with her presence."

"Whatever," Dani muttered. "I've never known you to be so eager to visit the track all the time, Kris."

"I could say the same thing about certain other people in this car," Kris countered, shooting Amber a glance as she climbed into the backseat beside her.

"Chill, ladies," Junior said as he put the Porsche into gear. "All kidding aside, Kris hasn't been to see Wildfire in days. So cut her some slack, Dani."

"Oh, please!" Amber rolled her eyes dramatically. "Like *Wildfire's* the one she's going to see!"

"What's that supposed to mean?" Kris snapped. "Of course I'm going to see Wildfire."

"Uh-huh." Amber leaned back against the car's leather seat with a smirk as Junior peeled out onto the quiet country road. "Sure. And that hot little number Logan has *nothing* to do with it, right?"

Dani laughed, glancing over her shoulder at Kris and Amber. "Right," she said. "I'm sure all that pathetic flirting was just her way of being polite. Not to mention the truly sad way she was throwing herself at him at that party last week."

"Why do you two even care who I flirt with or don't?" Kris said sharply. "Unless maybe you're jealous that Logan isn't interested in *you*, that is."

"Ladies, ladies!" Junior broke in before Dani or Amber could answer. "We're going to the racetrack, remember? If you wanted to go do some mud wrestling, you should have told me."

"Ew," Dani said, shooting her brother an irritated glance. But at least his barb was enough to shut her up.

Kris flopped back against the seat, determined to keep her mouth shut, too.

Why does Dani have to be so mean? She's like that when Matt's around, Kris thought. *And Junior. And just about any guy who I even look at sideways. It just drives her crazy to see any guy show interest in me at all. Especially if she thinks he's supposed to be out of my league.*

Pushing back her hair, which was whipping around her face as the car sped down the road, Kris suddenly felt tired of the whole thing. She found herself wondering if life might be easier if she just followed Dani's stupid rules and stayed away from guys like Logan.

Maybe I *should* stick to hanging around people who are more like me, she thought with a stab of self-pity. Like Pablo and Melina. They understand where I'm coming from, because they're coming from the same kind of place. And they would *never* think someone was too good for me.

She almost immediately felt guilty for thinking that way. Pablo and Melina weren't the only people who accepted her as she was. There was Todd, for instance. He had made her feel welcome at Raintree from the first day she'd arrived. And Logan seemed to take her for who she was, as well. Even Junior did his best, though she sometimes wondered whether he had ulterior—i.e., romantic—reasons for making her feel welcome. Regardless, he did try and that counted for something.

When they finally arrived at the track, Kris let out a big sigh of relief. Now she could focus on something other than her racing mind. Junior flashed his owner's badge at the gate guard, then drove down the narrow side road to the backside parking lot.

As they climbed out of the car, Dani checked her diamond-studded watch. "It's getting close to race time," she told Junior. "We should probably head right over to Daddy's stalls if we want to see Lantana Square before he goes to the paddock."

"Sounds good." Junior nodded. "Want to tag along, Kris?"

"Thanks." Kris smiled at him. "But I think I'll meet you out front. I want to go see if Melina's working today."

"Well, look who's here!" Logan called out twenty minutes later, when Kris arrived at the Trenton shedrow. "Good to see your pretty face around, Kris. Did Melina con you into cleaning stalls for her again?"

Kris smiled as Melina popped her head out of a stall and stuck her tongue out at him. "Actually, I volunteered. I just can't get enough of shoveling this stuff."

"Everyone needs a hobby," Logan said. "So,

seriously, what brings you to the track today?"
He was wearing a long-sleeved, button-down
shirt, and as Kris explained about the Davises'
horse, he started undoing the buttons, revealing a white T-shirt underneath.

"What are you doing?" Kris interrupted
herself to ask when she saw him remove his
Rolex watch. "Did somebody start a game of
strip stall-mucking and not tell me?"

Logan laughed. "Hey, sounds like fun!" he
said. "But no—actually, I'm just preparing
myself to get soaked from head to toe."

"Uh-oh." Melina looked up from dumping
a load of soiled bedding into her wheelbarrow.
"Does that mean it's time for Charm's bath?"

"You got it." At Kris's confused look, Logan
laughed. "Charm is one of the horses I
groom," he explained. "She loves to get me
soaked to the skin whenever I bathe her. Last
time she grabbed the hose in her mouth and
smacked me across the face with it."

He peeled off his long-sleeved shirt and
hung it on a bridle hook outside an empty
stall. Then he hung his Rolex over the end of
the hook on top of it. Kris looked at the watch

in an attempt to avoid the temptation of staring at the muscles rippling in Logan's bare shoulders.

"Okay," Logan said. "Almost ready. Now I just have to get rid of these pants and shoes. . . ."

As he pretended to kick off his sneakers, Melina glanced out of the stall she was cleaning and rolled her eyes. "Please, spare us your nakedness," she said. "Some of us just had lunch."

"Okay, okay." Logan grinned. Still wearing his shoes and his pants, he headed off down the aisle. "Wish me luck with the Charmer," he called back over his shoulder.

"Good luck," Kris called. Then she glanced at Melina. "You guys always have so much fun around here. And Logan's a riot."

"He's a dork, but we love him." Melina hoisted the handles of her wheelbarrow, which was full, and let out a groan. "I think we need to start feeding these horses less. They're killing me."

"Here, let me dump it," Kris said. "One of the other guys was on mucking duty at Raintree today, so my pushing muscles are well-rested."

Grabbing the wheelbarrow, she pushed it down the aisle, taking a shortcut around a couple of horses walking by. On her way, she spotted a familiar-looking light chestnut face peering out at her from one of the stalls.

"Hey, lady," she called out to the horse, recognizing Technicolor Rose. She set down the handles of the wheelbarrow and flexed her arms, giving her muscles a rest. "Guess you're back from that other track, huh? I'll have to remember to ask Melina how you did in your race." She scratched the filly on the jaw, then hoisted her wheelbarrow and moved on.

A few minutes later she pushed the empty wheelbarrow back the same way. As she rolled around the corner, she almost ran straight into Parker. He was standing in front of Technicolor Rose's stall staring at the filly.

He whirled around at Kris's approach. "You!" he barked out, jabbing a finger in her direction. "Did you unlatch this horse's door?"

"Huh?" Kris shook her head quickly. "Of course not! What are you talking about?"

"I just walked by as Rose was about to

break out of her stall." Parker glared at her. "Someone had undone the lower latch—I barely caught her in time!"

"Well, don't look at me." Now that she'd recovered from her surprise, Kris's temper flared at the accusing look in the assistant trainer's eyes. "Why would I open the stall?"

"*Someone* did." Parker's gaze was icy. "And here you are, just happening past the scene of the crime. Again."

"Your point?" Kris's voice was rising. She was getting pretty sick of his insinuations. "That doesn't mean anything. Why would I try to let your horse out?"

"Why did someone hide those blinkers last week?" Parker countered. In comparison to Kris's heated exclamations, his voice remained deadly calm. "Why did someone lift that bottle of Bute?"

"I wouldn't know!" Kris shot back. Realizing her hands were shaking, she tightened her grip on the wheelbarrow. "I had nothing to do with that!"

"Hmm." Parker was silent for a moment, though he continued to stare at her through narrowed eyes. "Well, from what I've seen and heard, trouble seems to follow you around."

"What's that supposed to—" Kris started to say, but she cut herself off. It was no use. Parker had already turned and stalked off down the aisle, disappearing around the corner to the right.

She slumped in place, suddenly feeling defeated. What had Parker meant by that last comment? Were her earlier worries right? Had he heard about her past?

Just then, she heard a cry from the aisle where she'd left Melina working a few minutes earlier. "Oh, great," she muttered. "What now?"

Dropping the wheelbarrow, she hurried around the corner and found Melina standing in the aisle, pitchfork in hand and a worried expression on her face. From the opposite end of the aisle, Logan was hurrying over to her, a mahogany bay filly trailing along behind him at the end of a lead rope.

"What is it?" Kris asked breathlessly.

"It's Logan's Rolex," Melina responded, pointing to a hook. "When I came out of this stall, it was gone!"

"What?" Kris and Logan cried out at the same time.

Kris's gaze flew to the hook where she'd seen Logan hang his things. The shirt was still there, but there was no sign of the gold watch.

"It must have fallen or something," Logan said, not appearing terribly concerned. "Can one of you look on the floor underneath? I'd do it, but . . ." He gestured at the filly, who was trying to nibble on his shoulder.

"I'll do it." Kris hurried forward, scanning the dusty ground under the hook.

Just then, Joey, the groom Kris had met the night of the party, appeared around the corner. "Hey, who's yelling over here?" she complained. "You made Mo jump and almost squish me while I was doing up his legs."

"Sorry about that." Melina set down her pitchfork and walked over to help Kris look. "But Logan's watch is missing. It's expensive and I'm afraid someone might have walked off with it."

"Who would do that?" Joey asked. "You'd have to be pretty bold to walk right up and take something like that. There's always people around."

"She's right," Logan put in, pushing the filly away as she tried to slobber down the side of his face. "I'm sure it was just an accident. A horse could have knocked it down on its way past."

"Maybe." Melina didn't sound convinced. "But I didn't notice anybody going by with a horse while I was working in the stall over there. I might have missed hearing a person go by, I guess. But not a horse."

Kris kicked around the dirt, hoping for a familiar glint of gold. But there was no sign of the watch. "Check in that stall," she suggested to Melina, pointing to the stall to the left of the hook, where a gray horse was calmly munching on some hay. "I'll look in this one."

She entered the empty stall to the right of the hook, kicking at the straw bedding. But there was still no sign of the Rolex.

"It's not in here," Melina announced, backing out of the gray's stall. "I just don't see it anywhere."

"Maybe somebody saw it hanging there

and tucked it away for safekeeping," Joey suggested. "Someone should go ask Parker in case it got brought to him."

"Good idea." Melina's face brightened. "I'll go find him."

She dashed off down the aisle. Logan's filly had started prancing, and he was walking her in a circle in the aisle. "Good thing I didn't take off my pants like I was threatening, huh?" he commented to Kris. "If those disappeared, I'd really be in trouble."

Joey giggled, but Kris wasn't in the mood for laughing. This is crazy, she thought. First Parker accuses me of letting that horse out, and now this. I'm starting to wonder if I really *am* bad luck for this place.

A few moments later, Melina reappeared, followed by Parker and Amber. "What's going on out here?" Parker asked. "Logan, Melina tells me your watch is . . . Oh." He stopped short as he spotted Kris. "No wonder something bad happened." His face twisted into a sarcastic little smile as he added, "The jinx is still here."

Kris felt her whole face go hot. She opened

her mouth to defend herself, but then shut it. What would she say, anyway?

"It's no big deal, Parker," Logan put in quickly. "I shouldn't have left it sitting out like that. My bad."

"Yeah," Joey said. "No offense, Logan, but I can't believe you even wear that Rolex around the barn to begin with."

"A Rolex?" Amber, who had been standing beside Parker playing aimlessly with a strand of her own hair, suddenly looked much more interested in the proceedings. "It's a Rolex that's missing? Wow, that's bad. So wait, Parker, why did you call Kris a jinx just now?"

"Because," Parker said, "she always seems to be around when things go missing or other problems happen."

Amber shrugged. "Oh," she said, already going back to twirling her hair between her fingers. "Well, just 'cause Kris was a jailbird, it doesn't necessarily mean she's up to no good *all* the time."

Kris froze. "Gee, thanks for your help, Amber," she said sarcastically.

"No problem," Amber replied, completely missing the point. "I do what I can."

"A jailbird?" Joey glanced at Kris in surprise. "What does she mean?"

Logan looked startled, too. "Hold on," he said. "Let's not start throwing accusations around until we give Kris a chance to explain."

"Yes, Kris." Parker stared at her. "Why don't you explain?"

Everyone had turned and was staring at her now. Melina looked anxious, Amber looked smug, and everyone else looked confused or accusing. Kris stared wildly from one face to another, suddenly feeling like a cornered animal.

"Forget it!" she cried out. Suddenly her safe, happy haven at the track didn't feel like the same kind of place anymore. "Just forget it! I won't bother any of you ever again."

She raced off down the aisle at a run, ignoring the calls from behind her. At the end of the row of stalls she turned and ran up the next aisle, just wanting to put distance between herself and the questioning faces behind her. Halfway down the aisle, she saw

Beau's big, kind-eyed head sticking out of his stall watching her. But she ignored him, her legs pumping faster and faster.

Moments later, she was letting herself into another stall in a different aisle. "Oh, Wildfire!" she cried out in a choked voice, burying her face in the horse's bay neck. "Why does stuff like this keep happening to me?"

Curling his neck down, Wildfire nuzzled curiously at her back. Kris didn't look up, merely hugging him tighter as the tears began to flow.

She stayed with Wildfire for a long time, all her fears and anger pouring out. ". . . and I have no idea what could have happened to that watch," she told him after a while, stroking his neck as she talked. "I had nothing to do with it. But I guess my word is not enough for some people." She frowned and stared into the air above Wildfire's withers, picturing Parker's accusing glare, Joey's shocked gasp, and Logan's confused green eyes. "Will it always be this way, Wildfire?" she asked the horse with a half-sob. "Will people always jump to the worst possible conclusions about me, no matter how hard I'm trying to turn my life around?"

Wildfire let out a soft snort, but didn't have any answers for her. She sighed, feeling a little better for having finally had the chance to express what she had been thinking and feeling.

"Okay, boy," she told Wildfire. "Thanks for listening. For once, I'm really glad you're here at the track."

She wiped her eyes on her sleeve, then reached out to give the horse one last hug. As she wrapped her arms around his warm, muscular neck, burying her fingers in his mane, she smiled.

How could I ever think Wildfire wasn't my number one? she wondered, pressing her face deeper into his sleek coat. He always will be, no matter what. I can admire another horse without losing any of my love for this guy. And it doesn't matter if I compare other horses to Wildfire sometimes, or notice that they might be better than him at some things. The important thing is, Wildfire and I are soul mates.

Feeling better for a moment, she stepped back and gave Wildfire a scratch in one of his favorite spots. As his eyes half closed and his lower lip startled to waggle with pleasure, she smiled again.

Then she remembered the reason she was there in the first place, and her fingers slowed and her smile faded. There was no way she was going to be able to keep hanging around the Trenton barn if almost everyone there suspected she might be a thief or a troublemaker or even just a jinx.

"I don't know what I'm going to do, Wildfire," she whispered, running her hand down his warm nose. "And if I don't figure out how to fix things soon, I might as well kiss all my new friends good-bye."

Chapter Twelve

Kris let out a groan and opened her eyes. Sitting up in her bed, she glanced over at her alarm clock. One forty A.M. She was never going to get to sleep. She'd been in bed for almost three hours, but her mind hadn't taken the hint. It was still racing with everything that had happened that afternoon at the track.

Swinging her legs over the edge of her bed, she stood up and wandered down the narrow trailer aisle to the door. When she opened it, she saw the familiar landscape of Raintree frosted in the bright, pale light of a full moon. The sound of a horse snorting drifted to her on a slight breeze, and she felt herself relax slightly.

I'll take a walk, she decided. Maybe that will clear my head.

Slipping on a pair of rubber muck shoes, she stepped out of the trailer in the boxers and tank top she'd worn to bed. The fresh, cool air and the peaceful sight of horses grazing in the distance didn't chase her worries away entirely, but they did help slow down her racing mind.

I think I know what's really bothering me about all this, she mused as she wandered along the fence line of the nearest pasture. Up until Logan's watch went missing, I was assuming that all the problems around Trenton's barn were just plain old bad luck. Everyone said that Rosie was an escape artist. A dog could've moved those blinkers, like someone suggested at the time, or torn open that feed bag. Even the missing Bute could've been lifted by a sneaky groom from another barn.

She paused as she reached the end of the fence line. Then she sighed and turned, ambling down the hill. With the moon out, it was almost as bright as daylight, which meant she didn't have to worry about watching her step. Unfortunately, that meant she was free to focus fully on her own thoughts.

But someone had *stolen* Logan's watch, she told herself as she continued to ponder the situation. No question about that. A dog or horse couldn't have reached it where he left it—only a person. And Parker, at least, seems to think that person is me.

Biting her lip, she felt a wave of frustration and helplessness wash over her. The only thing worse than being seen as a jinx was being seen as a thief. If she wanted to clear her name, she needed to figure out who really swiped the watch. But how was she supposed to do that?

Anybody wandering past could've seen the opportunity and taken it, she thought hopelessly. With Melina busy in the stall and nobody else around, there's no way of ever knowing who it was. Not unless someone can teach the horses to talk.

She looked up and noticed that she was

approaching the weanling pasture. Drifting to a stop, she smiled despite her worries. A pair of weanlings were romping around shaking their heads and playfully kicking out at each other. The rest of the herd lifted their heads briefly to watch the pair's antics, then returned to dozing. With the moonlight illuminating the horses, it was easy to make out Gent's swayed old back among the limber, leggy forms of the young horses.

But wait, Kris thought as she caught a flicker of movement over near the gate. If Gent and the weaners are over there, what's that?

She squinted and took a few steps closer. The mass of bodies just inside the fence near the gate shifted and separated into individual forms, only slightly smaller and more slender than the weanlings across the field.

Suddenly, things clicked into place in Kris's head. "Deer!" she cried out. "It was the deer!"

Her outburst startled the creatures. They leaped into motion in a whirl of legs and white tails, bounded over the pasture fence, and disappeared into the shadows at the edge of the trees that bordered Raintree's fields.

Kris watched them go, smiling at her discovery. The little herd of deer had been huddled around the damaged spot on the fence, and seeing them there, Kris suddenly knew exactly what they had been doing.

They've been coming down to slurp up the juice and stray chunks of apple that the horses have been drooling all over the fence when Todd feeds them, she thought joyfully. They must be nibbling at the fence in the process, making it look like a horse has been cribbing on it. I can't wait to tell Pablo.

As she turned and headed back toward her trailer, her heart felt a little bit lighter. Maybe she wouldn't be able to clear her own name after all that had happened at the track. But at least she could clear Gent's.

"Have you seen Pablo?" Kris asked Matt the next day when she came across him sorting feed receipts in the stable office. "I've been looking everywhere for him."

"Oops!" Matt glanced up at her with a guilty

expression on his face. "Sorry, I was supposed to tell you. He took the rig out to deliver that yearling we just sold downstate. Said he should be back later this afternoon."

"Oh. Okay." Kris was disappointed, but she could wait a few hours to tell Pablo about Gent.

Gent's rep will recover as soon as Pablo finds out the truth, she thought. Mine, on the other hand? If I don't figure out what to do about it soon, my rep could be ruined for good, at least around Trenton Stables.

She turned to leave the office, but Matt put out a hand to stop her. "Hey," he said, standing up and looking down at her with concern. "If there's something urgent, I'm sure Pablo has his cell on if you want to try calling. . . ."

"It's not that." Kris kicked at a stray bit guard lying on the dusty floor. "I was just thinking about something."

"Must be something serious. Your face looks all squinched up and grim." Matt smiled and touched her gently on the arm. "Anything you feel like sharing?"

Kris was about to say no, but then thought better of it. Two heads were better than one;

maybe Matt could help her figure out what to do. "Well, since you asked . . ." she began.

Matt listened without interruption as she told him about the recent events at the track. He already knew some of it, of course, but Kris didn't leave anything out. She needed him to understand why she was so upset about this.

". . . So, of course, Parker looks at me like he already had me tried and convicted in his own mind," she finished, her cheeks growing hot as she remembered the assistant trainer's glare. "And I'm sure everyone else over there is starting to think the same way. I have got to figure out a way to prove I didn't take that watch—and the only way I can think of is to prove who *did*."

"Wow, that's complicated." Matt stroked his chin, looking thoughtful. Then he glanced at his watch. "Look, I have some free time this afternoon, and I was thinking about driving over to the track to catch a few races, anyway. I can take you over there if you want to start investigating, or whatever."

Kris hesitated. After what had happened the day before, the last thing she felt like doing was showing her face at the Trenton shedrow. Then again, she wasn't going to make any progress trying to clear her name by hiding out at Raintree.

"Give me an hour to dump and scrub the water tanks in the fields?" she asked. "My other chores are finished, but I promised Pablo I'd take care of that today."

"I'll do better than that," Matt replied. "If I help you with the water tanks, we should be able to finish in half an hour."

Kris grinned. "Deal!"

Exactly thirty-five minutes later, the two of them were in the cab of Matt's truck, pulling through Raintree's gates onto the road. Kris was nervous about going back to the track, but she was doing her best to ignore the butterflies in her stomach. She was determined to do any-thing she could to clear her name. As Matt accelerated, she stared out the window. A storm system was rolling in from the north, and the afternoon had grown overcast and breezy. The air coming in through the truck's half-open windows felt chilly and moist.

Kris nervously glanced down to check her

watch. They would be at the track in just a few minutes.

"What am I supposed to do when I get there?" she murmured to herself.

She didn't realize, however, that she'd spoken the words out loud until Matt glanced over. "You mean about this missing watch thing?" he asked.

"Yeah. I mean, if some wandering stranger just happened by and took it, there's no way I'm going to be able to track it down and prove what really happened. Not with the millions of people wandering around the backside all the time."

"You're probably right about that," Matt said. "But that's not the only possibility you're looking at here, you know."

"What do you mean?"

Matt shrugged, rolling down his window the rest of the way and leaning his elbow on the frame. "You've got to admit," he said, "it does seem kind of weird that you're always around when things go wrong."

Kris frowned. "Look, I thought you knew me well enough by now to know I'm not a thief," she began hotly. "If you're seriously telling me you think I did all that stuff, you might as well stop this truck right now so I can get out and—"

"Whoa!" Matt briefly lifted both hands off the steering wheel in a gesture of defeat. "Chill, girl! Let me finish, okay? I'm not saying anything like that—and, yeah, that's mostly because I *do* know you well enough to know you definitely didn't do that stuff. But anyone who didn't know you so well would have reason to be suspicious, since you were around when all the problems happened."

"Brilliant observation, Captain Obvious," Kris muttered, still riled up about what she thought he'd just implied.

"But the thing is, someone would have to be an idiot to be that obvious." Matt held up one hand and laughed. "And, no, I'm not calling you an idiot."

"Okay." Kris's temper was already subsiding. "But what *are* you saying? I don't get it."

"I'm saying it's awfully suspicious that these things only happened when people *knew* you were around. That might not be an accident." Matt looked over at her, his expression serious this time. "It might be because someone's actively *trying* to frame you."

Chapter Thirteen

Kris was struck silent as Matt's comment sunk in. Someone framing her? It seemed so made-for-TV movie. But the more she thought about it, the more it made a strange kind of sense.

"You could totally be right," she said, thinking aloud. "Someone could be trying to make me look bad with the spilled feed and the other minor stuff, so then if something big goes wrong and I'm around, I'll get the blame." She grimaced. "Guess that means more people than I thought must know about my past."

"Maybe." Matt shrugged. "Or maybe they

just saw you as a nobody kid from a rival barn who might make a handy scapegoat."

"Right. And who makes a better scapegoat than the girl who just got out of the joint?" Kris shook her head, wondering why she hadn't thought of the framing idea herself. It was just the sort of plot that some of the other inmates at Camp LaGrange would concoct. "That makes it really easy for people to point at me when things go wrong. Sort of like Pablo automatically blaming Gent 'cause of his cribbing history."

"Huh?" Now it was Matt's turn to look confused by the conversation.

Kris quickly filled him in on the fence issue, though she left out the "juice" comment she'd overheard. She still didn't want to believe Pablo would have said anything like that.

"So it turns out Gent didn't have anything to do with it at all," she finished. "But Pablo and your mom seem all ready to ship him off for it, anyway."

"Okay. But they haven't, have they? And that story just goes to show that it's not always the obvious person who's guilty," Matt pointed out. "Sometimes, it's someone you didn't even consider."

Kris nodded and glanced at him, suddenly nearly overwhelmed with a flash of gratitude. Leave it to Matt to try to help me figure this out, she thought. I can always count on him when the chips are down. Sometimes I wish . . .

She stopped the thought before it had hardly begun. There would be no wishing for more between her and Matt. She had more than enough on her plate—romantically and otherwise. Instead, she tapped her fingers on the armrest, focusing hard on the watch problem. If she wanted to save her reputation around Trenton Stables, she needed to track down the real culprit. But who was it?

"I really hate to think that any of the people I've met at the track could have done something like this," she said. "They all seem so nice and not thieflike."

"I'm no detective," Matt said as he expertly swerved around a fallen branch in the road, "but I think you've got to just forget about how nice people are and make a list of *anyone* and *everyone* who could have done this. You know—the ones who were around when the stuff happened."

"You're right." Kris sighed and started ticking off names on her fingers. "There's Melina, of course. She was the one with the easiest access to that watch. But there's no way she would ever—"

"Focus!" Matt warned with mock sternness. "Just the facts, ma'am."

"Fine." Kris rolled her eyes. "So Melina, and Logan, and Parker were usually somewhere around. Not that Logan would steal his own . . ." At Matt's raised eyebrow, she left the last comment unfinished. "Um, who else? Let's see, Mac Mackenzie was usually around, and Shorty, Joey, Jackson, and José—oh! And I just thought of one more person who was there for some of the big stuff, including the watch disappearing." She turned to Matt, suddenly certain that she'd figured it out. "Amber!"

"Amber?" Matt repeated dubiously. "Why would *she* steal that watch? She could afford to buy herself a new Rolex for every day of the week."

Kris waggled one finger at him playfully. "Now, now, now," she scolded. "You're the one who just said to focus on who *could* have done it and not anything else. Amber was nearby; she could have walked by and grabbed the watch when no one was looking as easily as anyone else. And she certainly has a history of trying to make me look bad."

"Okay," Matt said, still not sounding convinced. "I guess you might as well leave her on the list. Now, tell me about some of these other—"

But now that Kris had come up with her Amber theory, she wanted to follow up on it right away. "There's no point going to the track if all our top suspects aren't going to be there, including Amber," she blurted out, cutting off Matt. She reached over and tugged on his sleeve. "Turn around—we've got to go to the Davis ranch."

"What? Why there?" Matt said. "How do you know Amber's even visiting Dani right now?"

"I don't. In fact, chances are she's not. But we need to invite Dani along to the track with us. Otherwise, Amber might get suspicious when we just invite her." Kris's eyes widened as she got another idea. "Oh! Unless you wanted to pretend you had the hots for her, or . . ."

"Forget it." Matt stomped on the brakes and then spun the wheel, executing a neat U-turn on the deserted road. "Let's just go and get Dani."

By a stroke of luck, Amber *was* visiting Dani when they arrived. The two girls had been chased away from the pool by the cool, cloudy weather and were now sitting in the Davises' spacious kitchen, trying to convince Junior to make them fruit smoothies.

At first, both Amber and Dani seemed disinclined to join Matt and Kris for their trip to the track, though Junior quickly accepted the invitation. But when Kris casually mentioned that she was planning to hang out at the Trenton shedrow with Parker and Logan, both of the girls had a sudden change of heart. Soon, all five of them were crammed into the cab of Matt's truck. Junior had managed to finagle the spot beside Kris, and for most of the ride she was distracted from Dani and Amber's annoying chatter by the way Junior's hand kept wandering over to rest on her leg.

Focus, girl, she chided herself, wriggling her leg to knock his hand off for about the fifth time and shooting him a dirty look that he returned with a sly grin. You've got way more important things to think about, she thought. For instance, even with Amber and the rest of our suspects at the track, how am I supposed to prove she—or anyone—did it? They make it look easy on TV: the detective finds a few clues, and then the bad guy just starts confessing. But somehow I doubt that's going to happen in this case. . . .

Slapping away Junior's hand yet again, she glanced over at Amber, who was laughing at something Matt had just said. The easiest way to prove Amber's guilt was to wait for her to commit another crime and catch her in the act. But what if she'd just taken that Rolex on a whim, and never had the urge to do such a thing again? Or, what if Kris had been right in the first place, and the watch had been lifted by a passing stranger? There were just too many unknowns.

By the time they reached the track, Kris still had no idea what she was going to do. Before the others wandered toward the grandstand so Junior could buy a program for that day's races, Kris promised to meet them at Trenton's barn in a few minutes. She had one stop to make before setting her investigative plan into motion.

"Hey, Wildfire," she whispered a moment later, ducking under the stall guard.

Wildfire had been taking a drink out of his water bucket. At her arrival, he lifted his head and snorted, spraying droplets all over her.

She giggled, stepping forward to wipe her hands and the arms of her windbreaker dry on the horse's shoulder. "Is that your way of saying you're glad to see me?" she asked. "I can't stay long—I have something really important to do. But I wanted to stop by and see you first for good luck."

With a snort, Wildfire shoved gently at her

with his head. "Sorry, no treats today," Kris told him, patting her jeans and jacket pockets to make sure. "I forgot. Besides, you probably shouldn't have too many snacks now that you're in training. I'll make it up to you when you get home, okay?" Oblivious to Kris's comments, the horse continued his search, sniffing at her back jeans pocket and then suddenly pulling up his head. When Kris looked, she saw that he had her laminated track license in his teeth. "Hey, give me that!" she cried with a laugh, snatching back the license before he could start chewing it. "If you eat that, they won't let me on the backside anymore." She tucked the license into her jacket pocket and zipped it shut for safekeeping.

After a few more minutes of bonding time, Kris forced herself to give him one last pat and leave the stall.

Here goes nothing, she thought.

As she walked over to the Trenton shedrow, the sun broke through the clouds, raising the temperature by several degrees. Kris shrugged off her jacket when she arrived at her destination, pausing just long enough to drop it on a spare hook in the deserted feed stall before moving on in search of people.

She found Melina in Technicolor Rose's stall working on the filly's already gleaming coat with a rubber curry in one hand and a stiff brush in the other. "Hi, Kris," Melina greeted her with a smile. "You're back! I was afraid after what happened yesterday . . . " She shrugged. "Never mind that. What's up?"

"Not much. Just thought I'd stop by for a visit, since I was here seeing Wildfire," Kris replied, giving the filly a pat on the nose.

"Did I see those oh-so-lovely friends of yours wandering around?" Melina's sunny expression darkened briefly. "That blond girl was hanging all over Parker. As usual. It's so pathetic how she throws herself at him, if you ask me."

"Yeah, they're here, too. So, um, I think I'll go say hi to some of the others. You know—like Shorty . . ."

Melina looked surprised. "Oh, okay," she said uncertainly. Then her face cleared. "Oh, and last I saw, Logan was scrubbing buckets over in the next aisle. Just in case you were wondering." She winked playfully.

Kris was confused for a second. Then she realized that Melina thought she'd mentioned saying "hi" to the others as an excuse to go flirt with Logan.

Just as well, Kris thought as she hurried off, embarrassed that her attraction to Logan was so transparent. *No matter what Matt says, I'm sure Melina didn't have anything to do with this. But it's probably better if she doesn't know I'm checking up on her friends and coworkers. At least, not until I figure out if it was one of them, or Amber, or someone else altogether. . . .*

She sighed, momentarily daunted by the task in front of her. *How did those TV detectives make it look so easy?*

Because that's just TV, she reminded herself. *This is real life. My life. And like Pablo's always telling me, I'm the only one who can make it better for myself.*

Just then, she looked up and saw Mac Mackenzie rounding the corner toward her. The slim, young exercise rider raised a hand in greeting, but his normally friendly expression remained guarded. "Hi there, Raintree girl," he said. "What are you doing here?"

"Just visiting." Kris kept her voice light, though it wasn't easy. Even though Mac was smiling at her, it was impossible to miss the cloud of suspicion in his eyes. She found it hard to believe that the cheerful, funny Mac could have anything to do with the theft. But remembering Matt's advice earlier about not ruling people out, she decided she might as well start her investigation right then and there.

"So," she said, feeling awkward as she fell into step with the exercise rider as he continued down the aisle. "How's it going, Mac? Anything new and exciting in your life?"

Mac glanced over at her, surprised by the questions. "Same old, same old," he said carefully. "Why do you ask?"

Kris winced. I guess I can't blame him for sounding wary, she thought. It's not like I ever showed any burning interest in the details of his life before now.

"No reason," she said, desperately trying to

sound normal. "I just realized you and I haven't really had a chance to get to know each other that well."

"Hmm." Mac tapped the riding crop he was holding against his leg. "Okay. Look, I don't want to be rude or anything, but I have a horse to ride right now. Catch you later, okay?"

"Sure." Kris stood and bit her lip as she watched him hurry off.

Okay, that didn't work, she thought. *I seriously doubt I'm going to convince any of these people to confess just by asking them stupid questions like that. Especially when they all seem to think I'm the one to be suspicious of. Maybe I need another approach. . . .*

She noticed that she was standing right in front of the open door to the Trenton tack room. As always, the converted stall was packed not only with tack, but also with all the other odds and ends and boxes of spare parts and equipment that went into running a racing barn. As she stared at the controlled chaos filling every corner of the small space, Kris realized that if someone wanted to hide something—say, a stolen Rolex watch—where nobody was likely to find it, the tack stall would be just the place.

Maybe whoever took it stashed it in here, Kris thought with a flash of hope. *If I could find it, maybe track security could dust it for fingerprints or something.*

It seemed like a long shot, but she wasn't eager to continue her pathetic attempts at interrogation. She stepped into the tack stall and lifted the flap of the closest saddle.

While she methodically searched the saddles, lifting each one to peek underneath as well as checking under the flaps, she thought some more about whether any of her suspects had really had the opportunity to frame her.

Melina couldn't have done it, Kris thought as she replaced an exercise saddle on its rack. *I mean, she could have grabbed the watch, I guess, but she was with me when Rosie escaped the first time, and also when the feed got spilled. So there's no way she did that stuff to frame me.*

Then there's Logan, she thought. *I can't imagine why he'd try to get me in trouble, especially by stealing his own watch. But more*

196

importantly, he was with us during the feed spill, too. So it couldn't have been him trying to make me look like the bad guy. . . .

She was digging through a bucket of loose metal buckles and snaps a few minutes later, still running over the various suspects in her head, when she heard footsteps outside the doorway. Glancing over her shoulder, she saw Parker standing there with Amber clinging to his elbow.

"Hey," the assistant trainer barked out. "You. I heard you were hanging around again. What are you doing in here? Looking for something else to steal?"

Kris's face burned as Amber giggled. "Oh, Parker!" Amber exclaimed in a lilting voice. "Are you still on that? Let it go already. If Kris did steal that Rolex, it's long gone by now." She smirked at Kris. "She has connections, remember? P-R-I-S-O-N."

"Congratulations," Kris spat out at the other girl. "It's nice to see you finally learned to spell. Did you grow another brain cell? The first one will be happy to have the company."

Amber rolled her eyes. "Grow up, Kris," she

began. "If all you can do is insult people—"

Parker's angry voice interrupted her. "Don't bother trying to talk to her, Amber," he exclaimed, his eyes flashing fire. "I've had enough. It's time to put a stop to this, once and for all. I'm calling track security to have her kicked off the backside—and if I have anything to say about it, she'll be banned for good!"

Chapter Fourteen

Kris let out a gasp of horror. "You can't do that!" she cried, taking a step toward Parker, her fists clenched at her sides. "You don't have any right to kick me out. I haven't done anything wrong."

"Oh, really?" Parker shook Amber's grip on his arm loose long enough to pull his cell phone out of his pocket. "We'll just see what security has to say about that. . . ."

"What's going on in here?" said Matt, who had appeared in the doorway behind Parker. "What's with all the yelling? Kris? You okay?"

Kris shrugged. "I don't know," she said, her voice dripping with sarcasm. "Why don't you ask Parker? He seems to think he knows everything about me."

"Huh?" Matt looked confused and worried. "Look, seriously, guys. What's going on?"

"Parker caught Kris looting this place," Amber replied, waving a hand toward the tack room. "So he's getting her banned from the track."

"Whoa!" Now Matt just looked alarmed. "Look, Parker. Let's be reasonable here."

"Impossi—" Kris began, but snapped her mouth shut at Matt's stern glare.

"I'm sure this is just one big misunderstanding," Matt said soothingly to Parker. "How about if we all just back off to our corners for a while and cool off?"

Parker scowled. "Why should I let her go?" he said, his voice still belligerent. "If she's stealing from me . . ."

"Kris, turn out your pockets," Matt said.

Kris's jaw dropped. "Are you kidding me?" she cried. "I'm not going to—"

"Kris!" Once again Matt cut her off before she could finish. "Just do it, okay? It's easier than standing here arguing about it."

Kris glared at him, suddenly feeling as if she were back at Camp LaGrange, where every move she made was watched. How could Matt talk to her like that? How could he take Parker's side against her?

"Go on, Kris," Amber taunted. "You know how to do it. I'm sure they frisked you all the time in juvie."

"Shut up, Amber," Matt said. He pushed past Parker and took Kris by the arm. "Listen," he murmured. "Just go with me on this one, okay? Trust me."

Kris narrowed her eyes. Did he even realize what he was asking her to do? He's not the one who had to put up with the daily humiliation of being stuck in a place like Camp LaGrange, she thought. He has no idea what it's like to be treated like a suspect day after day.

Still, she reluctantly reached down and pulled her front jeans pockets inside out. "See? No saddles hidden in here," she said bitterly. Kris next turned so they could see the back of her jeans. "Any supervaluable stirrup leathers sticking out of there?"

"Whatever. I don't have time for this,"

Parker said, checking his watch and then returning his gaze to Kris. "Just stay out of my tack room, or I *will* have you kicked out of here."

With that, he spun on his heel and stalked off. "Parker, wait for me!" Amber squealed, rushing off after him without a backward glance.

As soon as they were gone, Kris collapsed against the wall, her breathing raspy and fast. Matt stepped closer, putting a hand on her arm.

"You okay?" he asked tentatively. "Sorry for sounding kind of harsh, but I was just trying to—"

"Forget it." Kris brushed away his hand. "It doesn't matter. The important thing is that you stopped Parker from calling security. I get that."

Matt licked his lips, still looking uncertain. "Okay," he said. "But I'm still sorry."

"Whatever. Let's get out of here before Parker comes back and freaks out on me again." Kris headed out of the tack room, then stopped and glanced around. The sun was hidden behind the clouds again, and a cool breeze wafted down the aisle, making her shiver. She thought about going over to the feed room in the next aisle to get her jacket, but decided there was no time for that. She had something more important to do.

"Come on," she told Matt. "Let's go find Amber."

Matt blinked. "Amber?" he said. "Why? We just got rid of her, remember? And I, for one, am in no huge hurry to see her again."

"Believe me, I'm not thrilled about it, either," Kris said, already hurrying off down the aisle. "But how else am I supposed to prove that she's the one framing me?"

"What?" Matt jogged forward to keep up with her. "I figured you were joking when you mentioned her before. What makes you so sure Amber's the one?"

"Didn't you hear her back there?" Kris fumed. "Looting, my butt! She's *still* trying to make me look guilty in front of her idiot crush Parker. And she's loving every second of it!"

"Hold on a sec," Matt said, grabbing her

elbow and whirling her around to face him. "I don't blame you for being mad at Parker. The guy's kind of a jerk. But, come on—you can't seriously blame Amber for any of this! I'll be the first to admit she can be annoying, and I know you two don't get along that well. But why would she want to frame you for something like this? And really, do you honestly think Amber is even smart enough to understand how framing somebody works?"

"Are you going to help me, or not?" Kris asked as she pulled free of Matt and rushed around the corner into the next aisle, where José was carefully wrapping Beau's legs.

Matt caught up within a few strides, though he waited until they were past the horse and groom before responding to Kris. "You know I'll help you," he said once José was out of earshot. "But I really think we should keep investigating everyone. Not just Amber."

"Fine. You investigate whoever you want. It'll be better if we split up—less suspicious that way." Kris started off, then paused and glanced back at Matt. "Speaking of suspicious, where's Dani?"

"She and Junior got bored and went out to watch some races," Matt replied.

"There you go," Kris said triumphantly. "Dani's bored, yet Amber stays here without her? How suspicious is that?"

"Not very," Matt said. "Did you not notice her drooling over Parker just now?"

"Parker's just her cover story," she said. "I mean, think about it. He's sort of cute, but he's nowhere near tall enough or rich enough to interest Amber for more than ten seconds. Logan I could see, maybe. But Parker? No way."

Ignoring Matt's continuing protests, Kris hurried off in search of Amber, leaving him behind. Parker's office was her first stop. But when she got there, it was empty. A moment later, Kris spotted Parker emerging from the feed stall alone, with no Amber in sight. Kris moved on before Parker could notice her and finally tracked Amber down in the next shedrow. She was standing in the aisle watching Technicolor Rose pick strands of hay out of her haynet one by one and drop them on the ground.

Kris ducked into an empty stall nearby, pressing herself against the doorjamb and hoping Amber hadn't spotted her. She waited, remaining as silent as possible, until the other girl moved on. Then she followed her, still trying to keep out of sight.

That proved more challenging than she might have expected. For the next twenty minutes or so, Amber wandered aimlessly all over the shedrows, pausing to pat a nose here and watch a passing horse there. Kris managed to keep her in sight, ducking from stall to stall and even hiding behind a handy gelding at one point.

As Kris ducked behind a stack of hay bales, Amber finally left the shedrow and angled across the open area beyond. Kris realized she was aiming for the women's restroom between two sets of barns. She waited until Amber disappeared through the door, then hurried over. Holding her breath, she pushed open the door slightly. Not seeing Amber at the sinks in the otherwise empty restroom, Kris decided she must be in one of the stalls along the back wall. She stepped inside, planning to hide in another stall until her quarry emerged again.

"So you *are* following me!" an accusing voice greeted her.

Kris stopped short as Amber stepped out from behind the door. "Wh-what?" Kris stammered. "I was just coming in to, uh, wash my hands."

"Give it up, Kris," Amber snapped. "You're not anywhere near as subtle as you think you are. Why don't you just leave me alone already? It's pathetic! If you're that jealous of my relationship with Parker—"

"Huh?" Kris blurted, dropping all pretense of innocence. "What are you talking about? This doesn't have anything to do with that loser."

"Don't call him that," Amber said. "And don't even pretend you don't know what I'm talking about. It's totally lame how you're always throwing yourself at all these cute guys. First, Matt and Junior, now Logan and Parker—even someone as clueless as you must know they're totally out of your league."

Kris didn't answer for a second. Her head was spinning—and it wasn't because of

Amber's insulting comments, which were fairly typical.

Wait a second, she thought. Amber isn't really acting like I caught her at anything here. She's acting more like she caught *me*. And I know she's not much of an actress so I doubt she is trying to fool me.

She bit her lip, suddenly wondering if she'd been going at this all wrong. Maybe she should have listened to Matt when he questioned why Amber would frame Kris.

She certainly didn't set me up so she could steal that watch for the money, Kris thought, the logic gears in her brain belatedly switching on. And if she really wanted to frame me for some reason, she could've done a much better job of it. She easily could have planted the Rolex in my trailer, or something. And, yeah, she tried to make me look bad in front of Parker just now, but even that makes perfect sense—in Amber World, anyway—if she thought I had the hots for him.

Her heart sank as she realized she had to go back to the drawing board. Meanwhile, Amber was still glaring at her, her arms crossed over her chest. "Well?" Amber demanded. "Are you going to say something, or just stand there with that stupid expression on your face?"

"Excuse me," Kris mumbled, turning and heading back out the door. She didn't have time for Amber's drama right now.

"Hey!" Amber emerged from the restroom as Kris hurried back toward the shedrow. "I'm not finished with you yet!"

Kris ignored her, increasing her pace. Her mind was searching frantically through her list of suspects, trying to figure out which one might be the culprit. She was so caught up in her own thoughts that she was halfway down the aisle before she noticed Parker standing in front of Beau's stall.

It was too late to turn and go the other way—he'd spotted her. "Hey!" he yelled. "Do you know something about this?"

"What?" Kris asked. When she got close enough to have a clear view into the stall, she saw Beau standing there as calmly as ever. But the standing wraps she'd seen José applying earlier were now lying bedraggled and tangled around the colt's front legs.

Kris wrinkled her brow, confused. "What happened to his bandages?" she asked.

"That's what I wondered as soon as I saw him like that," Parker replied, his voice growing louder. "Then I looked in the stall and saw this." He held up a laminated card.

Kris leaned closer, then gasped. "My ID!" she cried, her hand automatically flying to the back pocket where she usually kept her track license. "How did you get that?"

Then her heart froze as she remembered that she'd zipped the ID into her jacket pocket after Wildfire had tried to eat it earlier. The jacket that she'd then left in the feed room, from which she'd seen Parker emerging soon after their argument . . .

"You!" she gasped as the truth hit her like a runaway racehorse. "You're the one who's been doing all this!"

Parker smirked. "I don't know what you're talking about," he said. "All I know is that someone came in here and sabotaged this horse, and your photo ID was lying in the straw right next to him."

Kris opened her mouth to argue, then

snapped it shut again. It was suddenly all too clear what had happened. Parker had come upon her ID in her unattended jacket and decided to plant it at the scene of her latest alleged crime.

That will look like solid proof to just about anyone, Kris thought, feeling completely helpless. And it will be my word against his. With Amber running around telling everyone about my past, who are most people going to believe?

Just then José appeared. The groom took one look at Beau's legs and gasped. "What happened?" he cried. "I just finished wrapping him thirty minutes ago and put him away clean and tidy!"

Parker stared at Kris. "Interesting question, José," he said. "Kris and I were just discussing it."

"Ay-yi-yi!" José exclaimed at the top of his lungs, seeming much more focused on Beau's bandages than Parker's answer. He let loose with a torrent of loud Spanish as he bent down to rip off what remained of the bandages.

José's shouting must have traveled

throughout the barn because a moment later, Melina, Logan, Mac, and Jackson all came running from various directions. "What's going on over here?" Melina asked breathlessly, still holding the rub rag she must have been using on a horse. "I haven't heard José swear that way since Joey spilled that entire bottle of Cowboy Magic on his lunch last month."

"Yeah." Mac glanced in at the horse. "Hey, what's up with Beau's wraps?"

Jackson stepped forward for a look. "What a mess," he stated after seeing the wraps. "José, that doesn't quite look like your usual wrapping job."

That comment brought another round of bilingual swears from José, who was still working on fixing the bandages. Jackson held up both hands and stepped back as the others chuckled.

All the while, Parker just stood there and watched the events unfold. Kris had the feeling he was waiting until he had everyone's full attention before speaking up. Meanwhile, she felt rooted to the spot, wishing she could run away but knowing it wouldn't do any good.

He's got me, she thought, white-hot frustration making her arms and legs shake. He's got me right where he wants me, and he totally knows it.

She glanced around, hoping Matt would turn up and save the day again. But the only person approaching was Amber, hurrying toward them from the general direction of the restrooms.

"I've finally figured out who's behind our run of bad luck around here," Parker said, his voice loud, confident, and clear. "Not just the loose horses and missing equipment, but also Logan's stolen watch and the petty cash that disappeared from the office earlier today."

Kris blinked in surprise. She hadn't even heard about the missing cash, though most of the others were nodding.

"The person behind it got sloppy, like guilty people always do. See, José wrapped Beau's legs half an hour ago and then left him alone. When I happened by and saw that someone had wrecked his wraps, I also found this in his stall." Parker held up Kris's track license, then pointed to Kris accusingly. "It belongs to her.

And if she did this, you can bet she's behind all the other problems too. Especially since nothing happened until she started hanging around."

There were several gasps of shock. Kris didn't even dare look over at Melina or Logan, or any of the others, to see the expressions on their faces. Instead she merely glared at Parker. But before she could speak up to defend herself, Amber shook her head.

"Don't be stupid," she told Parker matter-of-factly. "There's no way Kris could've messed up that horse like you said. She's been following me around like some demented bloodhound for the past half an hour."

"What?" Parker looked startled. "No, I'm sure you must be mistaken, Amber. She did it. I have the proof right here in my hand."

Amber shrugged. "Nope." She glanced down to examine the tip of one of her finger-nails. "I'm positive. She hasn't been out of my sight for the last half hour. If she'd stopped off to play with some nag's legs, I would've seen it."

Parker opened his mouth, then shut it

again. "B-b-but . . ." he stammered. Finally, he swallowed hard. "Well, that doesn't change the fact that stuff only started happening when she showed up, or that she's probably behind most of it, or . . ."

Logan glanced at Beau's legs, then stepped forward. "Look," he said, no trace of the usual joviality in his voice or eyes. "What's going on here, Parker? The *truth*."

"I'll tell you," Kris said, finally finding her voice. "He's been framing me all along so he could steal stuff and pin it on me. He took that ID out of my jacket and planted it so everyone would think I did this."

"She's lying!" Parker croaked, shifting his gaze rapidly from side to side as if looking for a way out. "Who are you going to believe—me, or some convicted criminal?"

There were murmurs from the others. Even José had stopped fiddling with Beau's bandages and was paying attention. Kris shot a glance at Melina and found her staring fixedly at Parker with a look of horror on her face. With a wince, Kris turned her attention back to Logan as he spoke up again.

"Keep an eye on him, will you, guys?" Logan said to Jackson and Mac. Then he turned and headed down the aisle. "I think I'd better go call Mr. Trenton—and track security."

Chapter Fifteen

"What did they ask you?" Kris asked as Matt approached the bench where she was sitting at the end of the Trenton shedrow. She glanced at the police officers standing by their squad car out in the open area near the restrooms. At the moment they were interviewing Jackson and Shorty, though they were too far away for Kris to hear what they all were saying. Several racetrack security guards were standing near the officers, along with a couple of official-looking men in suits.

Matt flopped down on the bench beside her. "Mostly a bunch of stuff about how well did I know Parker," he said. "And a few questions about the stuff that happened—whether I witnessed it myself or just heard about it, that kind of thing."

"Yeah, me too." Kris watched as two more security guards joined the group nearby. "I guess Parker must've confessed when they took him away, because it seemed like they were barely listening to my answers."

"He did confess," Matt said. "I heard Logan talking about it while I was waiting my turn."

"Really?" Kris sat up a little straighter, interested. It had been less than an hour since that final confrontation with Parker, and she was still trying to wrap her head around everything that had happened. "What did he say?"

Matt shrugged. "Well, I didn't hear every-thing," he said. "But it sounds like Parker was hoping to get back into riding. I guess he used to be a jockey, or something."

Kris nodded, remembering that Melina had said something about that. "What does that have to do with him framing me?"

"It sounds like he was having trouble getting back down to weight," Matt said. "A lot of
jocks have that problem—especially the ones
who are a little bit older. And a lot of them turn
to drugs for help."

"Yeah, I've heard about that," Kris said
sadly. She loved most things about the track,
but didn't like thinking about its hidden,
seamier side. "So Parker was using drugs to
get his weight down?"

"That's what it sounds like." Matt stared off
in the direction of the police car. "But that can
get expensive on an assistant trainer's salary,
and I guess he was getting desperate. So when
you started hanging around, and he heard
about your history, he figured that gave him
the perfect cover to start stealing to pay for his
habit. He must have thought making you look
guilty would be a piece of cake."

Kris shook her head slowly, amazed at how
deceitful some people could be. "But how did
he know about me?" she asked, not really
expecting Matt to know the answer. "Did he,
like, run a background check on me the first
time he met me, or something?"

Matt shrugged. "Dunno. Word travels fast around the track, though. Maybe he just heard it through the grapevine."

Kris didn't answer. She'd just noticed Melina standing a couple of aisles away with her arms wrapped around herself, watching the action out in the courtyard. Kris bit her lip, realizing the explanation was right in front of her. Melina was the only one who knew her history. Or, at least, she *had* been.

Just then, Melina turned her head and, catching Kris's eye, offered up a tentative half-smile.

Kris was tempted to turn away and ignore the other girl but instead, she climbed to her feet. "I'll be right back," she told Matt.

She hurried over to Melina, who was still watching her with that anxious half-smile on her face. But as soon as Kris reached her, the smile wobbled and Melina burst into tears.

"I'm so, so sorry, Kris!" she cried. "This is all my fault! I never should have opened my big mouth and told Parker you were in prison. . . ."

Kris clenched her fists, realizing she'd been right. As Melina rambled on, Kris just stared at her in silence, her mind racing.

I told her about my past in confidence, she thought. At least I thought I did. Obviously, she didn't feel the same way. She just used it as an excuse to flirt with Parker.

She felt fury building inside her, but she tamped it down. What good would it do? What was done was done, and at least everything had turned out all right in the end. And really, wasn't she was the last person who should be blaming someone for past mistakes?

"It's okay," she said at last, swallowing back the last scraps of anger. "You had no way of knowing what he'd do with that information. I just wish you hadn't told him."

"Me, too." Melina's tears had stopped. She swiped at her eyes with the back of her hand, looking miserable. "I—I just—it's so hard to know what to say to him sometimes, you know? To get him to really listen to me."

"I've been there." Kris nodded, her mind filling with images from the past. "Trust me, I know exactly what it's like to be desperate for attention, and to act without thinking. Growing up like I did—and you, too—it's hard to learn another way to cope sometimes."

"Yeah," Melina said softly. "I suppose that's true. But I'm still sorry."

There didn't seem to be much to say after that. Turning, Kris headed back toward Matt. She wasn't sure whether she and Melina would ever be friends like they had been. Too much lingered between them now. All she could do was wait and see what happened and believe that she handled it the best she could.

When she was about halfway back to the bench, she saw Logan hurrying toward her. She paused, and waited for him to reach her. At least one good thing had come out of all this drama—she hadn't really thought about Logan, or her feelings for him, in a while.

"Hi," he said when he caught up to her. "I was hoping you hadn't left yet."

"I'm still here," Kris said, feeling her breath catch at the intense way he was looking down at her with his clear, green eyes. "I wouldn't want to take off without thanking you for what you did. Standing up to Parker like that and everything."

Logan waved away her thanks, looking vaguely embarrassed. "Don't be silly," he said. "I knew all along that you had nothing to do with any of that stuff—especially taking my watch."

"That's nice," Kris said. "But you probably only felt that way because you didn't know the whole truth about me."

"You mean your prison record? Sure, I did." Logan smiled at her startled look. "Your friend Dani has a big mouth."

"She's not my friend," Kris said automatically, but her heart wasn't in it. She was too distracted by what Logan had just told her. He'd known all about her past—a past completely and utterly different from his own—and still believed in her. She couldn't believe it.

Maybe I shouldn't be so surprised, she thought, a warm and fuzzy feeling welling up inside. He has always been nothing but nice. Maybe I shouldn't have been so quick to assume that things could never have gotten serious between us. . . .

She realized that Logan was speaking again, and tuned in just in time to hear him say, ". . . and so I told them I could start right away."

"Huh?" she said, with the uncomfortable feeling she'd just missed something rather important. "What did you say?"

"I said, a trainer over at an East Coast track wants me to come work for him," Logan repeated patiently. "I'd be head groom to start, and then—well, we're leaving that open for now. But it could be my ticket to getting into training, and with some pretty nice horseflesh, too. Isn't that awesome?" He grinned, though his expression almost immediately softened as he touched her gently on the cheek. "The only downside is that I guess this is good-bye, at least for now."

Kris felt her heart sink.

"It sounds like a great opportunity for you," she told him, swallowing back the lump in her throat. "Good luck."

"Thanks." Logan smiled down at her,

looking impossibly handsome and happy. "Want to go grab a coffee to help me celebrate?"

"Thanks, but I'll have to take a rain check," Kris said. Logan was riding off into the sunset—literally—and she couldn't change that. It seemed easier to say good-bye now than drag it out any further. "I have to head home soon, and I really need to spend some time with Wildfire before I go."

Kris felt a little better after a nice, long visit with Wildfire, but the tension from the day's events lingered. She and Matt spent most of the ride back to Raintree in silence. When they got there, they were just in time to see Pablo backing the ranch's horse trailer into its parking spot. Kris suddenly remembered that she hadn't had the chance to tell him about Gent and the deer.

Pablo seemed surprised to see them pull in. "Hello," he said, swinging down from the cab of his truck as Kris and Matt climbed out of theirs. "Where have you two been? When I got back here, one of the grooms said you two had been gone all afternoon."

"We have," Kris said. "It's kind of a long story—I'll tell you all about it in a minute. First, though . . ." She went on to tell him what she'd witnessed the night before at the weanling pasture.

Pablo listened, nodding along. "A-ha!" he said, sounding pleased when Kris told him about catching the deer in the act. "That explains it. I'll have to ask Todd to be more careful."

Matt chuckled. "Sounds like a plan," he said. "I'll see you guys later, okay?"

As he headed up toward the house, Kris turned and fell into step with Pablo. "So aren't you psyched to hear that Gent's off the hook?" Kris prompted, a little surprised that Pablo didn't have anything else to say about the incident. "This means we can keep him, after all!"

"Keep him?" Pablo stopped and turned to look at her with a puzzled expression. "Who said we weren't going to keep him?"

"You did," Kris replied. "Um, I mean, didn't

you? Todd said he heard you and Jean talk-ing, and it sounded like you wanted to send Gent away if he was the one wrecking the fence."

"I see." Pablo turned and started walking again. "Well, Todd misunderstood. Kids do that sometimes."

Kris blushed, remembering the comment she'd overheard. Had she made the same mis-take as Todd? She didn't want to draw more negative attention to herself by bringing up what she had heard—not after the day she had had—but she also couldn't just let this drop until she knew the truth.

"Okay," she said, trying to figure out how to find out what she needed to know. "But you weren't just going to let Gent keep chewing the fence up, right? If he had turned out to be the one doing it, I mean. So what were you going to do?"

Pablo shrugged. "Lots of options," he said. "Cribbing collar, different field . . . Probably the easiest would've been to run an electric wire around the top of the fence. Then, juice it up with enough power to give him a good jolt the first time he touched it, and that would probably be enough to change his mind about cribbing there again."

"Juice it up . . ." Kris repeated. Her cheeks grew pinker as she realized that she hadn't misheard Pablo's comment, after all—but she had completely *misinterpreted* it.

I should've known he wasn't talking about the blue juice, she chided herself. Pablo would never put down a horse for something so silly. How could I ever have thought that?

"So are we done with all the hypothetical questions?" Pablo asked her with a twinkle of amusement in his dark eyes. "We've got a lot of hungry horses waiting for their dinner, you know."

"I know," Kris said. "I just—I'm just glad the mystery is solved. About Gent, I mean."

"I have to admit, I'd almost forgotten about it until you brought it up," Pablo said. "But I'm glad you figured it out, even if it wasn't really a big deal either way."

Kris smiled and nodded, though she didn't really agree. Pablo might not think it was a big deal, but she did. She hated to think of Gent

being accused of something he didn't do—
even if it didn't matter to anyone else.

And after all, didn't everyone deserve a second—or even sometimes, third—chance?

Turn the page for a
sneak peek of
Riding Lessons. . . .

WILDFIRE

Riding Lessons

An original novel by Catherine Hapka

Based on the series created by Michael Piller & Christopher Teague

"Good boy, Wildfire!" Kris Furillo cried, leaning forward to pat the big bay Thoroughbred she was riding as he slowed from a gallop to a canter and then finally broke to a brisk trot. Loosening her reins, she used her legs to steer the horse toward a dark-haired man standing by the gate of Raintree Horse Farm's practice track. "Pablo! That was an amazing ride," she exclaimed as adrenaline coursed through her.

Pablo Betart, Raintree's head trainer, nodded and glanced at the stopwatch in his hand.

"You both did well today. Less than half a second off the time I asked for. Nice job, Kris."

Smiling, Kris leaned down and gave Wildfire another pat while mentally, she gave herself a pat, too. Earning Pablo's respect (and his praise) meant a lot to her. After all, he was the one who'd spotted her working with Wildfire at a police-horse training center and recognized her raw talent with horses.

Kris had been there on a work program from Camp LaGrange, a juvenile detention facility where she was serving time for a minor car theft incident. But her rocky past hadn't stopped Pablo from offering her a job when she was released. He'd brought her to Raintree to work in the barn and learn horse racing from the bottom up. Pablo, unlike so many other people, had believed in giving Kris a second chance. For that (and his continued support), she was *extremely* grateful.

While Kris loved her new life at Raintree, it hadn't been the smoothest transition. The job itself involved long hours and lots of dirty, strenuous, and even dangerous tasks, none of which bothered Kris in the least. After all, she wasn't afraid of hard work. But figuring out how to get along with the new people in her life? That was an entirely different type of work. The ranch's owner, Jean Ritter, had been wary of Kris's past at first and had kept a close eye on her newest employee. Jean had been warming up recently, but Kris knew that could all change quickly.

To complicate the drama even further, Kris was still figuring out where she stood with Jean's teenage son Matt and his friends—especially Junior Davis, who lived on a neighboring ranch. Junior and Matt had both set their sights on Kris early on. Though Kris's heart was nudging her closer to Junior all the time, she still worried over whether her feelings—and his—were real.

But nevertheless, all the anxiety was worth it for the feeling of satisfaction she got from living on the beautiful ranch and working with horses all day long. That, and getting to be near her number-one love—Wildfire—who had come to Raintree along with Kris, and now was in training to be a star racehorse.

Snapping back to reality, Kris jumped down

from the saddle and ran up the stirrups. "Guess it was a good idea to keep Wildfire home for a while instead of sending him back to the track," Kris said. "He seems really relaxed and happy here."

"That's true," Pablo said, squinting at her in the bright California sunshine. "But it's not the main reason he's home. Jean wants him to stay through the Week of Winners."

"The what?" Kris said. "Oh, wait—is that the carnival thing you guys were talking about the other day?"

Pablo nodded, stepping back to loosen Wildfire's girth while he answered. "The Raintree Annual Week of Winners. I guess you could call it a carnival," he said. "But it's more like a local equine festival. We've been holding it every year here at Raintree for a long time— Jean's ex-husband was still around when the tradition started. Half the town always shows up, along with plenty of tourists."

"Sounds like fun," Kris said.

"It's a good time for the visitors, but a lot of work for us," Pablo warned. "So just prepare yourself."

"Got it." Kris unhooked her riding helmet and pulled it off, luxuriating as her long, dark hair tumbled free. "But wait, what does that have to do with Wildfire staying here instead of stabling him at the track?"

"Jean's hoping to use Wildfire as an extra draw this year," Pablo explained. "He's become a bit of a local celebrity since he won that claiming race so convincingly. People still remember how he ended up here, and you know how it is—everyone loves a Cinderella story like that. A wild horse saved by a head-strong girl? The local news has been all over it."

Kris nodded, her heart swelling with pride and amazement as she thought back to the recent events that had led up to this "celebrity" status. First, Wildfire had ended up at an auction after washing out of his police training. He'd been headed to slaughter before Kris found him at the auction and horsenapped him. The result? A police chase followed by some more time back in juvie. But Wildfire had been saved, so in Kris's mind, it was well worth it.

And then, just when Kris *and* Wildfire seemed to be getting back on their feet, Jean had been forced to enter Wildfire in a claiming race to pay off a huge tax bill. Every horse that raced was for sale for a fixed price to any qualified purchaser. Kris had been heartbroken at the thought of Wildfire leaving Raintree. In fact, she'd been so upset, she even convinced Junior Davis to put in a claim on the horse in the name of his father's stable. Asking him to do that had cost her more than she had expected. Getting Junior's help meant putting her own heart on the line . . . and her pride. The only way he would agree to the claim was if she spent the night with him.

Luckily, in the end it hadn't come to that. Junior's bid had lost out to another buyer—Pablo. The quiet trainer knew Wildfire was too good to lose and so had put up the money. Now he and Jean owned Wildfire in partnership and continued to race him under Raintree's silks.

When you think about it, Wildfire and I both had a pretty tough start in life, Kris thought, rubbing the horse's jaw as he nuzzled at her dark hair. But at least now we both have people who believe in us.

Pablo had finished fiddling with Wildfire's tack and turned to gaze at Kris seriously. "Listen, Kris, I wasn't kidding about the work," he said. "I know this is your first Week of Winners, so I want to make sure you understand that it's going to be a real upheaval of regular life. From now until after the event there will be no time for days off or—"

"Hi there! Are you Mr. Betart? Jean said I'd find you here!"

Kris and Pablo both turned at the new voice. A beautiful blond woman, a smile plastered on her face, was hurrying across the grass toward them. She appeared to be in her early twenties, and her flawlessly styled hair and makeup and her beige linen business suit looked as out of place on the dusty practice track as Kris's casual ponytail and grungy jeans would have been in a corporate meeting.

"I'm Mr. Betart," Pablo said. "And you are . . . ?"

"Jennifer Towers," the woman said brightly,

sticking out her hand. "But just call me Jenny, okay? I'm the event planner Jean hired to help put together WOW this year."

"WOW?" Kris asked.

Jenny turned her bright smile toward Kris. "That's what I've been calling it," she said with a giggle. "Week of Winners—WOW. Get it? Like, wow!"

"Nice to meet you, Jenny," Pablo interrupted, carefully wiping his hand on his jeans before shaking Jenny's hand. "You can call me Pablo."

"Pablo." Jenny smiled at him, cocking her head slightly to one side. "Cool name! Anyway, Pablo, I'd love to pick your brain about a few things. Do you have a second?"

"Sure, no problem. Kris, you can take care of Wildfire, right?"

Without waiting for an answer, he hurried off with Jenny. As they disappeared into the barn, Kris absently patted Wildfire.

"I never knew Pablo liked blondes," she commented to the horse, amused by how distracted the normally unflappable Pablo had seemed by Jenny's sudden appearance. "She seems a little young for him, don't you think?"

Wildfire let out a snort, spraying her with horse snot. Kris laughed and jumped away. "Thanks a lot, big guy," she exclaimed. "Let me guess—that's your way of saying Pablo is acting silly *and* it's time for your bath? Point taken, let's go."

A few minutes later, she was hosing down Wildfire in one of the barn's wash stalls when Matt appeared. "Hey, Kris," he said, running one hand through his tousled dark hair. "Sorry I didn't get to see Wildfire's workout today. How'd he do?"

"Great." Kris turned off the hose and glanced over at him. "Pablo seemed really pleased with the way he worked. Oh! And he told me Wildfire is one of the star attractions at this Week of Winners thing."

Matt chuckled. "Yeah, I heard Mom say something about that," he said. "I'm sure the finest families will be flocking here from miles around to . . . What?"

At Matt's curious "what," Kris realized that at his mention of the "finest families," she had grimaced—big-time. Matt was so down-to-earth that it was easy to forget that they came from totally different worlds . . . at least until a comment like that reminded her. As much as she hated to admit it, Matt was racing royalty and she was only a barn rat.

"Sorry. It's nothing," she said with a sigh as she began to unhook Wildfire from the crossties. "I was just thinking about how out of place I felt at that big horse party at the Davis ranch—remember? I know I was just there to work, but I still felt really weird just being there with all those dressed-up rich people. . . ."

"Don't worry, the Week of Winners is nothing like that," Matt assured her. "It's totally casual. Maybe even a little too casual."

"What do you mean?"

As Kris led Wildfire out of the wash stall, Matt fell into step beside her. "I keep telling Mom we could make more money with a few new ideas," he said, his expression taking on the intense look it always got when he was thinking hard about something. "I mean, half the money we make goes to charity as it is—"

"Really?" Kris asked. "Pablo didn't mention that part."

Matt glanced at her over Wildfire's back and nodded. "Yeah, we give half our profit to the retired jockeys' fund every year," he said. "We used to give them all of it. But these days . . ."

He let his voice trail off, but it wasn't hard for Kris to guess what he was thinking. It was no secret that Raintree had been struggling financially for the past few years. All over the farm changes were being made to cut back—from less expensive hay to taking on more paying boarders. It was also why Jean had entered Wildfire in the claiming race, and why everyone was now pinning their hopes on his racing career.

"So what kind of new ideas are you thinking about?" she asked, tugging on the leadline as Wildfire stopped to sniff at a stray pile of hay in the aisle.

"Things that would make it more of a big event instead of just a local get-together," Matt said. "Like maybe having a formal dance on the last night, where people can get dressed up and see and be seen."

Kris wrinkled her nose. "Now it's sounding like a Davis Farms party again."

"I guess that's sort of the point." Matt shrugged. "We already have pony rides for the little kids and carnival games and stuff like that. Adding the dance would offer something for people who are looking for a classier event—or even just an excuse for a fun night out. I'm sure it wouldn't hurt Raintree's business to get a few more of our well-heeled neighbors over here to check out the facilities, maybe get interested in some of our yearlings and two-year-olds in training, who will of course just happen to be around all groomed up and looking good. . . ."

Kris nodded, impressed by Matt's plans. He had a way of seeing the big picture that would make him a perfect owner—if he ever felt like taking on the responsibility. "Okay, makes sense," she said. "So what are some of your other brilliant ideas?"

Matt smiled, leaning back against the wall as Kris led Wildfire into his stall. "I'm glad you asked," he said. "See, I've been thinking—it's called the Week of Winners, right? So I think we should play up the whole horse racing theme even more than we already do. We already have the pony rides and a few racing demonstrations and things like that. But we could push it. Maybe do stick-horse races for the kids, or even run a betting seminar."

Kris felt her face flush with color and turned toward Wildfire, taking her time unhooking his halter. Recently she'd overheard Matt arguing with a local bookie named Bobby about money and it had made her wonder. Was Matt having gambling problems? And if he was, could she do anything to help him? Unfortunately, she didn't have any answers. For now, it was just one more thing to worry about.

Lucikly, Matt was too busy listing his ideas to take notice of her reaction. ". . . and maybe let people race their dogs or bicycles or something out on the training track, with purses and everything," he said. Laughing, he added, "I was even thinking we could try to imitate a high-end Thoroughbred auction. Mom and Pablo probably won't let us actually auction off any of the horses. But maybe we could sell other stuff, like horse racing memorabilia or something."

"Hey, while you're at it, why not auction off people?" Kris suggested.

Matt blinked and shot her a half-smile, as if not certain whether she was joking. "Um, I'm pretty sure that's been illegal since, you know, the Civil War. . . ."

Kris laughed. "That's not what I mean, silly," she said, giving Wildfire one last pat before letting herself out of the stall. "I mean, like a bachelor auction. You know? I saw it on TV once—they get people to sign themselves up to be auctioned off as dates or whatever. People can bid to go out with them."

"I get it. I've seen that sort of thing on TV too, come to think of it." Matt rubbed his chin, starting to look excited. "Kris—you're brilliant! It's a great idea. We could still play up the horse theme by trying to get people to sign up to offer services like discounted horse training or whatever. Mom would probably auction off some riding lessons and pony rides. And of course, we can do the date thing, too—people might have fun with that."

Kris nodded. "It'll be totally entertaining to watch, and probably raise a ton of money, too."

"Yeah." Matt turned to gaze at her with a cocky smile. "So how about it, Kris? Are you going to volunteer to go on the block? Bet you'd get a lot of bids from guys wanting to go out with you."

"No way!" Kris said, shuddering at the thought. "I'll be spending the auction the same way I'll be spending the rest of this Week of Winners thing—watching from behind the scenes—where I belong."

To be continued . . .